"Why are you here?" Emma asked bluntly.

Because you make my mouth go dry. Because I've never craved a woman as much. "I would have thought it was obvious." Turner said. "I want to talk to you."

She reached down to pick up the nozzle of the garden hose, twisting it to shut off the spray of water. "What about?"

He started to take the hose from her hand. When she resisted, he tugged harder. Emma tightened her grip and held on, taking a step back and nearly tripping on her dog. Turner reached out to catch her, his arm snaking around her waist to keep her from falling, inadvertently bringing her close to his body.

For a moment the world disappeared as he looked into fathomless eyes that met his. Her moist mouth was only inches away from his, her body pressed hard against him. Turner shut his eyes and took a deep, ragged breath until he won the battle for control. Barely.

It didn't help when he felt her tremble in his arms. Or hear the husky desperation in her voice when she said, "Let me go."

"I don't think I can," he admitted, and knew it was the truth. . . .

WHAT ARE *LOVESWEPT* ROMANCES?

They are stories of true romance and touching emotion. We believe those two very important ingredients are constants in our highly sensual and very believable stories in the *LOVESWEPT* line. Our goal is to give you, the reader, stories of consistently high quality that may sometimes make you laugh, sometimes make you cry, but are always fresh and creative and contain many delightful surprises within their pages.

Most romance fans read an enormous number of books. Those they truly love, they keep. Others may be traded with friends and soon forgotten. We hope that each *LOVESWEPT* romance will be a treasure—a "keeper." We will always try to publish

LOVE STORIES YOU'LL NEVER FORGET
BY AUTHORS YOU'LL ALWAYS REMEMBER

The Editors

Loveswept®

614

Patt Bucheister
Stroke by Stroke

BANTAM BOOKS

NEW YORK · TORONTO · LONDON · SYDNEY · AUCKLAND

STROKE BY STROKE

A Bantam Book / May 1993

Bantam Books are published by Bantam Books, a division of
Bantam Doubleday Dell Publishing Group, Inc. Its trademark,
consisting of the words "Bantam Books" and the portrayal of
a rooster, is Registered in U.S. Patent and Trademark Office
and in other countries. Marca Registrada. Bantam Books,
1540 Broadway, New York, New York 10036.

Prologue

King Knight cranked open the leaded window in his study to allow in some cool fresh air. And to diffuse the clinging odor of a forbidden cigar. He was in too good a mood to have it altered by his disapproving housekeeper, who wouldn't hesitate to give him another long-winded lecture on the evils of the expensive cigars a satisfied client had given him. Alvilda Gump, like his late wife, Myra, had never understood the visceral satisfaction a man got from a fine cigar. King knew the cigar wasn't good for him, but at age seventy, he felt entitled to indulge occasionally in one of the few vices left to him.

The sound of a woman's happy laughter drew his attention to the two young people walking toward the stables. He lingered over the sight of his tall firstborn son and the young woman Michael was holding closely at his side. A smile of pleasure replaced King's frown, brought on by the thought of facing Alvilda's displeasure.

One down, three to go, he reflected.

The frown returned when he heard his housekeeper behind him, muttering, "Feeling proud of ourselves, are we?"

"As a matter of fact, I am." Turning, King saw Alvilda fan the air with her hand after setting a tea tray down. Her mouth was set in a thin line of disapproval, but the expected lecture wasn't coming out of it. He was going to get off easy this time.

"I was right about Michael and Cassidy being perfect for each other, wasn't I?" he said. "Are you ready to admit I know what I'm doing after all?"

Alvilda refused to concede defeat. "One success does not mean total victory," she said as she poured the tea. "You were just lucky with your first attempt at matchmaking. You have three children left and they are all as stubborn as you, so I wouldn't be getting too cocky if I were you."

"You need to have more faith, Alvilda. You have a very unhealthy attitude about things turning out for the worst."

Her cockney accent grew more pronounced as Alvilda argued with him. "While arranging the lives of your children, you haven't stopped to consider they might prefer the lives they've created for themselves without any interference from you."

"Oh, pooh," King said indelicately. "They'll all thank me for helping them find the person they need to make their lives complete. Michael has."

She shook her head in exasperation, automatically adding a dollop of cream and one cube of sugar to his cup of tea. "So who's the next victim?"

"Turner," he said as he accepted the cup from her. "I've already put things in motion."

"Who's the lucky woman?"

"I tossed out the prospects of the other women Turner knows after I read the detective's report on Emma Valerian. Actually there weren't all that many women to sort through, since Turner spends most of his time working. I'm hoping Miss Valerian will change that. She has a most unique background, and I have a good feeling about her. She's just the person to give Turner the necessary push the boy needs."

"The 'boy' is thirty-two years old, King. Don't you think he would like to choose his own mate?"

"He chose her two years ago when she came to work for him. He just hasn't realized it yet."

"If he hasn't done anything about her for two years, it doesn't sound like he's likely to now just because you're pushing her in his direction."

King was suddenly serious, all signs of humor and arrogance replaced by deep concern. "Turner needs someone to show him there is more to life than work. You saw him when he was here last month. He's working himself into a first-class ulcer trying to be the best damn lawyer there is. Ever since he was a young lad, he's felt he had to be the best he could be, at everything. For himself, not because he was in competition with anyone else. He needs to look closely at those scales of justice that symbolize his profession. They're supposed to be balanced, and Turner's life is too weighed down on one side with work."

"So you're counting on this Emma Valerian to balance out his life?"

The glint of humor was back in King's faded blue eyes. "I think Emma Valerian is the key to unlock that door Turner shut years ago when he decided to take up law instead of attending art school. If he was happy with his choice, I wouldn't think of interfering."

"Of course not," Alvilda said with an exaggeratedly pained expression. "I'm curious how you're going to change a situation that's existed for two years. It seems a bit like flogging a dead horse at this point. Why will summoning Turner here suddenly make him mad about a woman he's done very well without for two years?"

"It's not my summons that will shake him loose. It's what she's going to do."

"I don't follow you. What is she going to do?"

Counting on his fingers, he said, "One, she's handing in her resignation notice, which will make him realize he doesn't want her to leave for professional reasons and, hopefully, for personal ones as well. Two, he's getting pressure added by my request for his shield."

"How could you possibly know what this woman's plans are? You don't even know her."

"The detective I hired has ways of finding these things out." When he saw Alvilda's skeptical expression, he went on, "The detective doesn't ask me how I paint. I don't ask him how he detects."

"At least in Michael's situation, you knew the woman you were throwing at him. For Turner's sake, I hope you know what you're doing."

"From what I saw when my son was here for my birthday, Turner is burning the candle at both ends and in the middle. It's time for drastic action."

"And you expect this Emma Valerian to be able to change Turner's life. That's a tall order. Turner, like all of your offspring, is not the most malleable material to work with."

His gaze shifting to the view outside the window, King thought of his lovely late wife, whom he missed as much now as on the day she died. "I'm hoping Emma Valerian will fill the emptiness deep inside him as his mother did for me."

One

Several of Turner's professors in law school had implied there'd be days like this. Mondays were notorious for being a difficult day for most people coming off a pleasant weekend, but this particular one might go down in the history of Kimball and Knight, Attorneys-at-Law, as the most hectic yet.

At least from Turner Knight's point of view.

His partner was out of town, which left Turner taking panic phone calls from some of Harry Kimball's demanding clients along with his own share of business calls. The copy machine had broken down again, which meant that whoever needed something copied had to race up two floors to use the copier in an accommodating architect's office. To add to the joy of the day, the accountant for one of Harry's more valuable clients had just skipped town with a sizable chunk of money he'd skimmed off the client's account. Turner had enough of his own work piled up on his desk and credenza to keep him burning the midnight oil for the next two weeks. The Ferguson case alone represented hours of preparation. It was also the most important case he'd ever handled, and one of the most complicated.

Opening the narrow middle desk drawer, Turner used his thumb to separate an antacid tablet from what had been a full roll that morning. There were just a couple of tablets left, and it was only four in the afternoon. Maybe he'd better start buying them by the case, he mused as he popped the antacid in his mouth.

He glared at the two white sheets of paper lying beside each other on the oversized green blotter on his desk. They were the latest cause of the pain in his gut. Tugging the knot of his tie loose, he sighed heavily as he unbuttoned the collar of his white shirt.

He'd read autopsy reports that contained more pleasant details than the two documents in front of him.

One was a copy of a letter his secretary had removed from the fax machine an hour earlier and had immediately brought in to him. The letterhead was a familiar drawing rendered by his father of Knight's Keep, his father's stately home. A faxed message to Turner's office in San Jose, California, from King Knight's home in Somerset, England, wasn't all that unusual. In fact, it was a fairly regular occurrence. Turner was partly to blame for the steady tide of messages. He was the one who'd given King the damn fax machine for his seventieth birthday a month ago. Like a kid with a new toy, his father regularly fired off missives to his four adult children, and they usually contained subtle hints or blunt demands for them to change their single status and get busy breeding grandchildren.

This latest fax wasn't about ending Turner's bachelor existence, however. Nor was it as amusing or as easily dismissed as the others.

The letter next to it was typed on Kimball and Knight business stationery. The woman who'd composed it, typed it, and signed it worked for him. Or would for two more weeks. For a man who had a reputation for quick thinking and intelligent rebuttal in the boardroom and the courtroom, Turner had been stunned when he'd read the letter, which he'd found in an envelope propped up against the small clock on his desk when he'd returned from a business luncheon a couple of hours earlier.

He'd been furious when he read it a second time. Mystified when he gave it a third reading. Now he was back to being ticked off.

Emma Valerian was quitting her job.

He could manage without Harry and the copy machine, even his secretary temporarily. He wasn't so sure he could get by without his efficient paralegal permanently. With the Ferguson case and his other work, he didn't even want to try.

Turner stared at Emma's resignation, then at his father's letter. It was a toss-up as to which one contained the worse news. Both represented great inconvenience to him.

He set the message from his father aside for the moment to deal with Emma's typed resignation. He would like to wait until Harry came back from the trip he'd taken to New York to introduce himself to his new granddaughter. Turner was going to have to handle this one on his own, however, even though Harry would stand a better chance of getting Emma to change her mind than he would. His partner's affable nature could charm vultures into singing like canaries. All of the staff adored the senior partner of Kimball and Knight, including the stoic Miss Valerian.

The staff stepped more lightly around Turner, and he was aware of it. He knew he was considered a perfectionist and a workaholic, and he couldn't argue with this assessment. He was both. But he never asked the staff to work any harder or longer hours than he did himself.

Emma's conversations with him were limited mostly to the weather, unless they had to do with a particular case. Then she would rattle off the codes and the precedents that applied. Any attempt Turner had ever made toward a friendlier working relationship with her had been met with a subtle but definite return to business matters.

A door closed quietly, he'd concluded, was just as effective as one that was slammed shut when it came to keeping someone out.

This time she was going to have to give him more than a cold piece of paper, though. He wanted to know why she was quitting and what it would take to change her mind.

Pressing the intercom button on his phone, he said, "Linda, will you ask Emma to come in here, please? When she arrives, hold all my calls and anything for Harry."

"Yes, sir," answered the disembodied voice of his secretary.

Leaning back in his chair, Turner ran his fingers impatiently through his thick black hair as he tried to think of even one incident that would indicate

Emma wasn't satisfied with her job. Since she'd never once complained about the amount of work she handled, he had taken it for granted she was happy at Kimball and Knight. Obviously he was wrong. If she had other reasons for quitting, he wanted to know what they were. He couldn't fight an enemy he didn't know. And he was going to use whatever weapons were necessary in order to get her to stay.

What he needed were facts to back his position, arguments against her resignation backed by cool reasoning. As he waited it occurred to Turner that he knew little more about Emma than he did the day she'd been hired. Trying to figure her out over the past two years had been like reading an intriguing book with every other page missing.

He went over what he did know about her. She was twenty-six, single, and one of the most intelligent women he'd ever known. Professionally she was the best paralegal in the field. Her personal life, however, was a complete blank. Even though he'd worked with her almost daily for two years, he didn't have a clue about her life away from the office. She could have a live-in lover and six kids, or belong to a biker gang for all he knew.

He smiled. It was a stretch to picture the solemn Miss Valerian in black leather, although the thought had tantalizing possibilities. She had the slender hips and long legs that would complement sleek leather pants.

Turner frowned. He didn't like to think about the occasions in the past when he'd wondered what she would look like without any clothes on at all.

This time the clench of tension tightening his lower body couldn't be appeased by an antacid. The ache of arousal was almost as familiar as the burning discomfort in his stomach and stood just as much of a chance of disappearing if he kept thinking about Emma.

His mood didn't improve any when he tried to recall the last time he'd taken a woman to bed. A date didn't come to mind. He realized he couldn't even come up with a month or a woman's face and name. Although pathetic, the lack of sexual encounters made him feel better about his uncontrollable response to Emma Valerian.

At least he had a logical reason for his hormones sending out distress signals. He was thirty-two, not a hundred and two, with a healthy appetite for more than food. Due to the pressures of work, he'd been on a starvation diet for female companionship. No wonder his body hummed and hardened with desire whenever he thought of Emma, the only single woman in the office.

His strange obsession with Emma Valerian could also be ascribed to his tendency to choose a difficult course over an easy one. She was definitely a challenge.

The burning sensation in his stomach flared, and with a sigh of defeat, he reached for another antacid.

Emma stood on the other side of the door, staring at the gray paint that had been applied several months earlier during Mrs. Kimball's annual redecorating of the offices. She bit her lip briefly, nervously, and shifted her weight from one foot to the other.

This was ridiculous, she chided herself. All she had to do was reach for the doorknob, turn it, and walk in. She'd done it hundreds of times in the last two years.

Her hesitation was noticed by Turner's secretary, who was seated behind her desk several feet away. "He's expecting you, Emma," she prompted. "You can go right in."

Stalling, Emma asked, "What kind of mood is he in?"

"Somewhere between a grizzly with a sore tooth and a lion who missed his lunch two days in a row." Then Linda loyally added, "Harry's daughter could have chosen a better time to have her baby. Turner has enough of his own work to do without having to take on Harry's as well. From the amount of dictation tapes piled up on my desk when I arrived this morning, he worked all weekend again, which means he's worked fourteen days in a row."

And she had chosen that day to submit her resignation, Emma thought. Under the circumstances, she could have picked a more opportune time, but Turner wasn't going to like the inconvenience of working with someone new no matter when she quit her job.

It was easy for her to visualize the way irritation could turn his cobalt eyes to blue ice in an instant. Lord knows, she'd seen it happen often enough. In all the time she'd been his paralegal, she'd seen Turner in many moods, mostly demanding and short-tempered. She didn't expect today to be any different.

It was unfortunate the copy machine had broken down that same day, she reflected. That meant there were two office machines trying Turner's patience—the copier and her.

When she still paused in front of the door, Linda said, "You of all people know his bark is worse than his bite, Emma. Turner will give you enough work for three people, tell you he wants it done yesterday, you'll take the assignments, and somehow get it all done. Why would today be any different?"

Emma could have explained that her reluctance was due to her resignation, but she never discussed her personal decisions with any of the staff. It wasn't her nature to confide in people, and she certainly wasn't going to start now.

She faced the door again. This must be how criminals feel while they await their verdict, she thought. Turner's reaction could go either way, with him calmly accepting her two-week notice or stubbornly attempting to talk her out of it. She expected the latter. Experience warned her that the next few minutes were going to be extremely unpleasant, but putting it off wasn't going to make it any easier.

She lifted her shoulders in a slight shrug and gave the secretary a martyred smile, which she imagined resembled the way someone might look when she was about to have her head chopped off. Taking a deep steadying breath, she raised her hand and rapped a knuckle on the door once.

She heard Turner bark impatiently, "Come in, Emma."

Feeling as though her heart was lodged in her throat, she pushed open the door.

The woman who was on Turner's mind all too often walked in and said quietly, "You wanted to see me, Mr. Knight?"

His frown deepened. Emma was the only member of his staff who used his last name. Harry had always preferred an informal atmosphere around the office, and Turner had gladly gone along with it when he'd joined the firm as a junior partner. Emma had no difficulty using Harry's Christian name or being on a first-name basis with the other employees. She was only formal with him, and it irritated Turner every time she said "Mr. Knight" in that cool, distant tone of hers, as though he was someone she'd just met. And wasn't all that thrilled to meet.

"Sit down, Emma."

She glanced at the leather chair he'd indicated. "I'd rather stand."

"Black."

She looked utterly confused by his statement and glanced around in case she'd missed something. Bringing her gaze back to him, she said, "Excuse me?"

"I was waiting for you to say white," he drawled. "This will go a lot quicker if you don't automatically contradict everything I say and agree with me once in a while."

"Black," she muttered through clenched teeth.

A corner of his mouth curved upward in a mocking smile. "Ah, if your sweet compliance could only last." He held out the resignation she'd signed. "Take this," he ordered abruptly. "I'm not going to accept it."

Her arms remained at her sides. "If I took my resignation back, it would mean I intend to stay at Kimball and Knight. I don't. I am leaving in two weeks, Mr. Knight."

Turner gave her the patient look he reserved for stubborn clients. His voice became calm, yet firm. "You didn't state the reason you want to leave. Could you at least explain why you're taking such drastic action?"

"Drastic action?" she asked, her brown eyes widening in surprise. "I'm only quitting my job, Mr. Knight, not jumping off the roof. I would hardly call my decision drastic."

Turner disagreed. For two years she'd been the most reliable member of his staff, never complaining, her work impeccable. Her photographic memory saved hours of research, her ability to recall statutes and codes was phenomenal. He'd come to depend on her. Unlike the copier, she never broke down. Unlike his partner, Emma was always there.

Drastic wasn't the correct word for Emma leaving the staff. Disaster would be more appropriate.

A few minutes earlier Turner had been confident he could talk Emma out of resigning. Now he wasn't so sure. Leaning back in his chair, he looked at her long and hard as he pondered how to handle the situation. And as he had in the past, he ignored the sexual pull in her direction.

His initial attraction to her had been unexpected

and unwelcome the first day she'd reported to work at Kimball and Knight. He'd been astonished then by his body's response. He didn't like his reaction any better now.

Emma Valerian wasn't even close to being the type of woman he was usually attracted to, and he didn't understand why he reacted like a sailor on shore leave whenever he saw her. It was more like a moth being attracted to a match flame, he told himself. The women he chose to date didn't have to be raving beauties, but he did require them to be alive. There were times when Emma had all the animation and warmth of an ice cube.

"It won't work, Mr. Knight," she said softly.

"What won't work?"

"I'm familiar with your tactics. The silent treatment doesn't intimidate me."

"Is that what I'm trying to do? Intimidate you?" he asked with a hint of humor. "And here I thought I was simply struggling to figure out what will make you change your mind about leaving Kimball and Knight."

"Nothing will make me change my mind."

"You know better than anyone in this office that I hate to lose, Emma," he cautioned. "That doesn't just apply to court cases."

"You aren't losing anything, Mr. Knight. Someone else will take my place. You'll never notice the difference after a couple of days."

His gaze narrowed as he detected a note of sarcasm in her voice. Something was different about her today, but he couldn't put his finger on exactly what.

It wasn't her appearance. Unlike the other women in the office, Emma never wore slacks or even informal skirts and blouses. Over the past two years, Turner had noticed she basically wore three tailored business suits: a navy blue, a light gray, and one a tan color that reminded him of coffee with cream. He often thought of her suits as uniforms, though he had no reason for that strange notion. It was just as bewildering as his involuntary response to her.

Her blouses were either plain in light pastel shades, or patterned with narrow stripes or tiny flowers. She rarely wore jewelry other than small stud earrings. No rings adorned her long slender fingers, no bracelets encircled her delicate wrists, no flashy or whimsical pins decorated the lapels of her suits.

Today she was wearing the tan suit with a crisp white blouse buttoned up to her neck and fastened with a precisely folded bow. Every strand of her light brown hair was confined in a tidy knot at the base of her slim neck. Not once had he ever seen her wear her hair any other way.

Nor was there ever a time when he hadn't wondered how far her hair would fall down her back after it was released from confinement, or ponder how silky the strands would feel in his hands.

Her brown eyes were partially shielded by lightly tinted glasses with outsized clear plastic frames. Her makeup was almost nonexistent. As he looked at Emma he noticed how her skin glowed with health. That thought brought another, which made him tighten his fingers on the arms of his chair.

Good Lord, he was wondering how her porcelain skin would feel under his lips, whether it would be cool or warm, and how she would taste. Dammit, he didn't need this complication now.

Emma had never encouraged him or anyone else to look at her in a personal way, and it wasn't only because of how she dressed. Her cool manner kept people at a distance. He couldn't recall even one occasion when she'd spoken about herself, her life outside the office.

Which was fine with him. He didn't want to think about what he would do if she gave him the slightest encouragement. His policy of not mixing business with pleasure might not hold up.

Turning his attention back to the problem at hand, he smiled. A friendly approach occasionally worked with some of his toughest opponents. It was worth a shot now.

Emma didn't smile back. He hadn't expected any other expression on her face than the one she usually presented to him—solemn, cool, and professional.

"What's this all about, Emma? Do you want a raise? If that's the problem, just say so. You don't need to go through all this."

"Harry gave the entire staff raises last month, Mr. Knight," she reminded him. "I have no complaints about my salary. It's always been more than adequate."

Even her voice made him burn. "There has to be a way we can work this out. Tell me what you need, and it's yours."

Turner wondered if he had imagined the flash of anger in her eyes before she lowered her lashes. He mentally replayed what he'd said, but couldn't find anything that would make her angry. As he continued to stare at her she met his gaze once more with her normal detached expression.

"I believe the phrasing of my resignation is quite clear, Mr. Knight. It is the accepted form used to notify an employer when an employee wishes to give two weeks' notice before terminating employment."

"If you wrote it, Emma," he said dryly, "I have no doubt that it's correct. Your work has always been impeccable, which is one of the reasons why I'm hoping I can talk you out of quitting. We need you here."

"I'm not going to change my mind, but it's nice to know my work has been acceptable."

Turner's eyes narrowed as he caught the note of irony in her voice. There had been occasions in the past when he'd suspected she was secretly laughing at him, but he'd always dismissed that as ridiculous. Now he wasn't so sure.

He tried again. "Your work has always been more than acceptable, Emma. That's why it will be extremely inconvenient if you leave the staff at this time." He gestured with his hand to indicate the stack of files on his desk and behind him on the credenza. "You know how many important cases we have pending, especially the Ferguson lawsuit. This isn't a good time to be breaking in someone new."

"There will always be important cases, Mr. Knight," she said reasonably. "You won't have any difficulty finding someone to take my place. No one is indispensable."

"I don't agree. I can't imagine any other paralegal capable of filling your sensible shoes."

Turner had no way of knowing how hard his paralegal was fighting the urge to throw one of her *sensible* shoes at his head.

This time she didn't bother to disguise the flare of temper in her eyes, nor did she conceal the biting edge in her clipped response. "I didn't sign a contract when I started to work for Kimball and Knight. It's perfectly legal for me to quit my job."

Turner stared in fascination. It was like finding a boiling caldron where he'd expected to see still water. The temptation to discover what other passions she hid behind those tinted glasses was almost overpowering.

Frustration and growing desire hardened his voice and his body. "If you've been offered another job, tell me how much more they're willing to pay you, and we'll match it. We'll even raise it."

Her voice was suddenly cool enough to frost glass. "It isn't a question of money."

"Then what is it?" He leaned forward as a sudden suspicion insinuated itself through the heat of physical attraction. "Are you feeling all right, Emma? Are you leaving for health reasons?"

For a moment he thought she was going to laugh.

"I'm perfectly fine," she replied.

"You aren't getting married, are you?" Unintentionally he made it sound as though the very idea was ludicrous. Adding insult to injury, he added, "Or pregnant?"

"No," she said. "I'm not planning on getting married. Nor am I pregnant." She added sharply, "For someone who says he wants me to stay, you're making it easier for me to leave."

He knew anger wouldn't accomplish a thing. Yet as he pushed himself to his feet, planting his hands on his desk and leaning toward her, he couldn't control the harshness in his voice.

"Dammit, then why are you going to leave me, Emma?"

The color drained from her face, and she took a faltering step back. "What did you say?"

She couldn't have been any more surprised by his unintentional slip than he was. But once he'd put the thought into words, he realized he'd meant it. He was taking her resignation personally. That reaction was as bizarre as the sensual heat she aroused in him.

"I'm not blind, Emma," he said quietly. "I'm perfectly aware of how you feel about me, but I don't think it's a reason for you to quit your job. We can work around it, ignore it, or do whatever it takes to make you stay. Hell, I'll slide memos under your door. You won't even have to see me."

He didn't think it was possible, but she paled even more, then an embarrassed flush tinted her high cheekbones. For a few seconds she looked at him with a stricken expression before she lowered her gaze to the floor. Taking a deep breath, she visibly controlled her emotions and raised her long lashes to meet his intense gaze.

"Then you'll understand if I leave immediately rather than work out my two weeks, Mr. Knight."

"Will you stop calling me Mr. Knight?" he exploded, barely controlling the urge to jump over the desk and shake some sense into her.

He gasped suddenly as a slash of pain tore into his stomach.

"What is it?" Emma asked as she started to come around the desk.

Turner held his hand up to hold her off. "Don't. Just give me a minute."

She took another step closer when he sank down heavily onto the chair, holding his arm across his middle. "What can I do? Would a glass of water help?"

He shook his head. "No thanks." He pulled the middle drawer open and eased the last two antacids from the roll. "Something I ate for lunch didn't agree with me."

"Again? This isn't the first time this has happened, Mr. Knight. Perhaps you should go to a doctor, or at least change restaurants."

The pain was letting up, enabling him to smile. "See why I want you to stay, Emma? Who else is going to fuss over me like you do?" He sighed. "Now if I could ever get you to use my first name, I could die a happy man. We've known each other for two years. Maybe we aren't friends, but, dammit, we aren't strangers either."

She shook her head, a peculiar sadness haunting her dark eyes. "You don't know me at all, Mr. Knight," she said with quiet dignity. "That's not going to change no matter how long I work for you."

"Dammit, Emma. You belong here."

A bleak look crossed her face, then was gone. "I once thought I did, too, but I don't."

She walked toward the door, but before she opened it, she glanced at him over her shoulder.

"I'll finish the memorandum for the Milligan case before I leave today. I won't be back in the morning. Personnel can send my check without severance pay. Since I won't be working out my two weeks' notice, I won't expect it."

Turner stared at the door after she closed it quietly behind her, fighting the urge to throw something. Or go after her.

Had the whole world gone crazy, or just his little corner of it?

Two

The sound of rustling paper finally drew Turner's gaze from the door to his hands. He'd crumpled Emma's resignation. Tightening his fingers around the tersely worded letter gave him a great deal of satisfaction, since Emma's slender neck wasn't available.

Still, he was surprised by his violent reaction. Not only did he resent Emma's resignation, but he was actually feeling betrayed, and that was ridiculous. Other employees had left the firm before without it mattering to him, other than creating the nuisance of dealing with someone new who was unfamiliar with the way the office was run.

He let a new realization soak in. Part of his anger was because she was leaving before he had gotten rid of the odd fascination he felt toward her. *He* wanted to be the one to find a way to stop the magnetic pull so he could prove to himself he was in control.

In his professional and his personal life, he preferred order and consistency. He insisted on complete control of every aspect of his life, and he hated not being able to get rid of his attraction to Emma.

Even though his feelings for her didn't make sense, he'd managed to suppress his desire all this time. Why couldn't she do the same with her dislike for him and stay? How difficult could it be for her to set aside her animosity and continue to work with him? She'd managed it for two years.

Replacing Emma wasn't going to be easy. It might even be impossible. She was the most efficient paralegal he'd ever worked with, always supplying him with whatever he needed, and sometimes before he needed it. Her preparation of documents was perfect, her research detailed and clear. He depended on her faultless memory and the way she freed him from mundane matters.

And she turned his blood to molten lava just by walking into his office. Dammit, he was going to miss *her*, and it had very little to do with her qualifications as a paralegal.

Needing to stop thinking about Emma until his anger and his desire cooled, he picked up the message from his father. He read it again. Parts were clear, like the greeting.

HOW'S MY SECOND SON AND FAVORITE LAWYER? WORKING TOO HARD AS USUAL?

The rest didn't make any sense at all. King had written that he needed Turner's shield so he could take the Camelot chess set out of its specially constructed glass case. *To sell it!* But Turner wasn't to bring his shield to England until next week.

What the hell was his father up to? he wondered. Like his two brothers and one sister, Turner had been at Knight's Keep to celebrate their father's birthday just last month. King had been his usual self—arrogant, funny, a pain in the butt on the subject of not having any grandchildren, and in astonishingly good health for a man of his years. As usual he'd challenged all of them to a game of chess with the Camelot set, a tradition whenever they came for a visit.

Silver, his sister, was the only one who ever came close to beating King, but that was mainly because she didn't adhere to the unwritten rule of silence while the game was being played. Still, even when she'd gone into exaggerated descriptions of some of the propositions she'd received from stockbrokers, she'd failed to shake King's concentration entirely. He'd been fascinated by her colorful conversation, but he'd still won the game.

Not once during their visit had King even hinted he was thinking of selling the Camelot set.

Turner reached for the phone and dialed a series of numbers to place an overseas call. He would contact his father first, then his brothers and his sister if necessary. He pulled a legal pad in front of him and began to doodle on the top sheet as he waited for the call to go through the various interchanges. Ten minutes later he hung up.

Glancing down at the pad, he was startled to see Emma Valerian's eyes looking back at him. In only a few strokes of the pencil, he'd captured the sadness he'd seen briefly in her eyes and the Mona Lisa smile shaping her mouth. For a minute longer he indulged himself by adding some shading and more refinements to the sketch. It was an indulgence he rarely allowed himself.

But, Lord, it felt good. Each stroke of the pencil was sure, each line bringing Emma's delicate features into sharper focus with an expertise that hadn't dimmed from lack of practice. The hunger he tried to keep hidden deep inside to apply paint to canvas ate at him to bring Emma's likeness to life with color. He would use yellow ochre mixed with white and a touch of cadmium red light for a base skin tone. For her eyes, he would choose burnt umber and raw sienna with a light touch of cadmium yellow deep for the reflective glow he had seen occasionally in their depths.

He made a harsh sound that was both deep frustration and sharp inner pain. He snapped the pencil into two jagged pieces, then tore off the page he'd drawn on and crumpled it.

He'd made his decision years ago. It was too late to change it now.

Turner tossed the wad of paper and the broken pencil into the trash basket and leaned back in his chair. Forcing his mind away from the pleasure he'd gotten from creating Emma's image, he dwelled on the phone call he'd made a few minutes earlier.

His capacity for surprises had obviously been used up by the day's events. It had barely fazed him when his father's housekeeper had informed him that King wasn't there, then had told Turner he could talk to his brother Michael if he wished. Turner hadn't even thought it odd that his older brother was in England instead of on his ranch in Montana.

It was that kind of a day.

When Michael came to the phone, he told Turner that he was at Knight's Keep because he'd received the same message as Turner, only his had been an immediate summons. However, King had gone off on one of his sketching jaunts before Michael arrived, and Michael hadn't been able to talk to him yet.

After chatting for a few minutes more with his brother, Turner agreed to fly over to England the following week if Michael hadn't discovered why King would even consider selling part of their heritage. Like Michael, he wasn't going to give King his shield unless King came up with a sound reason for selling the Camelot set. He knew Ryder and Silver would feel the same way. King couldn't open the specially designed unbreakable glass case unless each of his children provided their individual gold shields. All four had to be in place along with King's for the locking mechanism to release the lock.

The intercom on his desk buzzed. Pressing the button to connect him with his secretary, he asked irritably, "What is it, Linda? I thought I asked you to hold all my calls."

"It's after five," she replied smoothly, unaffected by his gruff tone. "I'm ready to leave for the day, and I'm switching the phones to the answering service. You asked me to remind you of the Milligan case file. Emma has the memorandum ready. Would you like me to bring it in before I go?"

"Ask Emma to bring me the file." He wanted another opportunity to talk to her.

"She's not here, Turner. She left a few minutes ago." After a brief hesitation, Linda added, "She cleaned out her desk before she left and even took the small ivy plant she kept next to her computer. Instead of saying good night, she said good-bye."

Turner ignored the curiosity in his secretary's voice. Emma obviously had meant it when she'd said she was leaving today.

"I'll get the file later," he said. "Leave it on your desk."

"All right," she replied crisply, clearly not satisfied with his failure to provide information. "You might think about leaving yourself. You worked all weekend again. You know what they say about all work and no play."

"I've heard it once or twice. Good night, Linda."

After a defeated sigh, she murmured, "Good night."

Shifting around in his chair, Turner looked at the stack of case files he should be working on. Instead of reaching for one, he leaned back and stared out the window. Since his office was on the third floor, he didn't have much of a view except for the windows of the building next to his. It didn't matter. His mind had wandered to the variety of emotions he'd seen Emma display earlier. She'd been a different woman from the one he was accustomed to observing around the office.

It was as though the quiet brown mouse had been replaced by a snapping lioness.

Mixed in with his irritation with Emma for quitting was an unsatisfied curiosity about the woman behind the serious facade. The glimpse he'd seen of anger in her eyes had added fuel to the attraction that burned deep inside him.

Perhaps he had been guilty of treating Emma like a walking legal encyclopedia, but her attitude had never encouraged anything else. Now that he'd experienced the flare of her temper, he wanted to learn more about the woman underneath the tailored suits, large tinted glasses, and serious demeanor.

And black lace, he recalled suddenly. Once in the conference room, he'd caught a glimpse of delicate black lace caressing a shapely thigh before she'd adjusted her skirt after sitting down. Turner had found it necessary to push his chair farther beneath the table to conceal his immediate physical response.

The thought of Emma wearing sensual lingerie under those uniform suits only added to the mystery, to the attraction, and fired his imagination.

Turner pushed his chair back and stood up. The briefcase he always took with him remained on the long credenza as he walked out of his office. It would be the first time he'd ever left Kimball and Knight without taking work home with him.

He went directly to his secretary's desk and her Rolodex, ignoring the Milligan file. He gave the circular file an abrupt turn until he came to the section he wanted. VALERIAN, EMMA was the second card after the letter *V*, with her address and telephone number neatly typed underneath.

His gaze narrowed as he memorized her house number and street, a muscle clenching in his jaw. Miss Emma Valerian was going to give him an explanation about why she was so damned anxious to leave him.

This time he didn't bother mentally correcting himself. He was through kidding himself. This was personal.

After locking up the office, he strolled to the bank of elevators and stabbed the down button.

There was another answer he wanted from her, a more pressing one than her reason for quitting her job. For too long she'd been like an itch under his skin that he couldn't scratch, and it was driving him nuts.

One way or the other, he was going to get her out of his system.

Emma slid the cut-down cardboard box containing bedding plants over the grass, moving along behind it on her knees. Aside from the sound of children playing in the cul-de-sac of this housing development located at the base of one of the foothills of east San Jose, the only noise marring the peaceful evening was the soft growls coming from the lively, four-legged bundle of fur beside her.

A small, much-chewed teddy bear was dropped on the ground near where she was digging in the dirt. Emma picked the bear up and tossed it aside.

Her gray-and-white Shih Tzu scurried around her, snapped up the toy with her teeth, and returned to her original position beside Emma. This time the low growl was accompanied by a paw brushing her arm when Emma didn't react to the hint fast enough.

Chuckling, Emma said, "You're not helping one bit, Dragon. I want to get these plants in the ground before it gets dark."

The small dog made it clear she couldn't care less about gardening by growling a little louder. Emma tossed the stuffed toy over her shoulder.

She managed to plant all the colorful flowers, despite tossing the teddy bear at repeated intervals. From experience, she knew Dragon would keep insisting on attention as she did every night when Emma came home.

Standing up, she brushed off her hands on the thighs of her jeans, then picked up the hose that had been lying on the grass. She twisted the metal nozzle at the end, adjusted the spray, and directed the water toward the flowers she'd just planted, thoroughly soaking the freshly turned dirt.

The layout of flowers and shrubs didn't look exactly as it had in the picture she'd found in a magazine, but it was close. It didn't matter that she was the only one who would see the results at the back of her house. Well, it mattered sometimes, she admitted reluctantly, but it didn't seem as though her solitary life was going to change in the near future, if at all. She'd been on her own a long time, almost her entire life.

Thinking of her childhood always made her appreciate what she had. There were worse things than being alone.

The sun was low on the horizon, sending golden light over the backyard and the rear of her house. The neatly trimmed shrubs, the sparkling clean windows, the newly planted flowers gave Emma a great deal of satisfaction. The landscaping had taken many hours of hard labor to create, and it was worth every blister and sore muscle.

Each time she drove into her driveway, she felt a rush of possessive pleasure when she looked at the house. Her home. It was that simple and that profound. Home. The first home she'd ever had to call her own. She never took it for granted and doubted if she ever would.

If she could get Sadie to come live with her, everything would be perfect. Emma hated the idea of the older woman living rough when Emma could provide a safe haven. If it hadn't been for Sadie, Emma wouldn't have her home, her education, or even her name.

The little dog was no longer satisfied with playing by herself. Dragon scampered around Emma's legs, vying for her attention.

"Patience has never been one of your finer qualities, Dragon. We really need to work on that." She bent down to fondle the dog's ears. "It looks like I'm going to have time to do something about your manners after today. I won't be leaving you every morning as I have in the past, so you'll be able to bug me full-time. What do you think of that?"

Dragon barked and raced away across the lawn. Emma smiled at the dog's spirited antics. At least someone was happy she had quit her job. It hadn't been an easy decision to make, but leaving Kimball and Knight was the only thing she could do. Even if she hadn't made plans for the rest of the year, she would have looked for a position with another law firm.

Heat climbed up her neck to her cheeks as she recalled Turner's claim that he knew how she felt about him. It had been humiliating enough for her to be aware of her infatuation. She thought she'd been so careful not to let on to him or to anyone else in the office about her attraction to her employer, but to her horror, he'd known all along.

At least after today, she wouldn't have to face him again. There was some comfort in that thought.

It wasn't easy watching him work himself into the ground either. Just a few weeks earlier she'd overheard Harry advise Turner to lighten his work load, so she knew she wasn't the only one who'd noticed Turner was taking on too much for one man to handle. The extra hours she'd put in to ease his preparation time hadn't made any difference. There wasn't a single thing she could do except not be around when Turner eventually burned out.

She found herself remembering one of the bits of advice she'd heard often from the self-appointed sage who'd headed the last commune she'd lived in. "Always step forward. Never backward." As far as prophetic wisdom was concerned, Brother Thomas's advice wouldn't rank very high, but it applied in this instance.

On her own since age eleven, Emma had devoured thousands of books in order to learn how to live in normal society. Of all the books she'd read, however, she hadn't been able to find a single one that gave her instructions on how to stop being attracted to a man who thought of her as a walking law library.

Redirecting the spray of water, she enjoyed the sight of the sunlight turning the drops of water to gold. The hours of work and planning were finally paying off, and she was pleased with the results.

Not every project had turned out the way she'd hoped it would, but overall she had built a good life on a solid foundation, unlike the nomad existence that had composed her childhood.

She was brought back from her thoughts by Dragon. As she moved farther along the lawn she pulled the hose after her, making the long plastic tube writhe in the grass like a rubber snake. Dragon was fascinated. Clamping her tiny sharp teeth around the hose, the small dog started to shake her head vigorously and growl at the strange animal she'd captured.

Emma turned quickly to stop Dragon before the dog bit a hole in the hose. "You little rascal," she exclaimed, the amusement in her voice eliminating any chance of the dog taking her reprimand seriously. "Let go of that hose."

In order to reach for the dog, she had to drop the spray attachment onto the grass. Dragon squirmed out of her grasp, and Emma lost her balance as she lunged toward the dog and missed. The grass cushioned her fall, and she ended up sprawled on her back.

Her laughter was followed by a screech of surprise as she was drenched with cold water. Dragon bit down on the hose just below the nozzle and inadvertently directed the spray at her. With a shower of water hitting her in the face, Emma tried to grab Dragon again, but the dog wiggled away. Dragon backed up, her paws landing in the wet, freshly turned soil, the hose still in her teeth.

By the time Emma finally managed to grasp Dragon, her white cotton T-shirt was plastered to her breasts, she had streaks of mud on her face and arms, and several paw prints on her shirt and jeans. Wet strands of hair clung to her throat. Grass stains and dirt were smeared on her jeans.

Her laughter drowned out the sound of creaking hinges as the gate in her privacy fence was pushed open.

As she playfully tussled with her mischievous dog she was startled to hear a familiar male voice drawl, "You're the last person I suspected to be into mud wrestling, Emma."

She was too stunned by Turner's sudden appearance to do anything but stare at him. Dragon made up for her lack of response. The dog hopped off Emma's midsection and scampered across the grass to greet the new visitor. Most of the wet dirt on the dog's paws had been transferred to Emma, but enough remained to leave several muddy deposits on Turner's jeans.

Turner dragged his gaze from the woman sprawled on the ground to the fluffy object with four short legs. Dragon was greeting him in the way she greeted everyone, by jumping up and down and placing her front paws on whatever part of the person's anatomy was within reach. In Turner's case, it was just below his knees. Turner had no way of knowing Dragon would keep up the lively dance until she was acknowledged with at least a pat on the head, and preferably a considerable amount of petting. Luckily he responded in the approved manner by bending down, a long way down, to place his hand on the excited animal's head. He was rewarded with an assortment of pleased doggy sounds, a wildly waving tail, and a moist pink tongue.

Only vaguely aware of the dog's pleasure, Turner continued to fondle the little creature's ears as he brought his gaze back to Emma. Stunned and fascinated by the sight of his usually pristine paralegal dressed in a wet T-shirt and tight faded jeans, Turner couldn't help wondering if the T-shirt hugging her breasts belonged to a man she lived with. Then he realized the shirt would have to belong to a very small man or a young boy, considering the way it hugged her body like a tight glove. His gaze lingered on the compelling sight of her nipples pressing against the T-shirt, making it obvious she was wearing nothing underneath.

When she brought her legs under her and stood up in one graceful motion, he let his gaze flow over her from her bare feet to the mass of damp, tangled hair that surrounded her face. She wasn't wearing her glasses, and he was able to see that her eyes were the color of rich, dark coffee. The tiny stud earrings had been replaced by large golden wire hoops.

The office mouse had turned into an exotic gypsy.

This Emma was the most sensual creature he'd ever seen, and his body responded with a desire that made his previous attraction seem like a momentary heat flash. This Emma made his blood run hot and thick like molten lava, and made his breath drag in and out of his lungs as though he'd been running a marathon.

The other Emma had been a spark of attraction. This Emma was pure dynamite.

She seemed equally curious about the differences in his attire, and his heart rate quickened as she slowly examined his jeans and emerald-green shirt.

To get his mind off wanting her hands to run over him with the same intensity as her eyes, he gave the dog one last caress and straightened.

"Could I see your driver's license?" he asked.

She blinked in surprise. "Why?"

"This is Emma Valerian's address, but you don't look anything like her."

She acknowledged his comment with a faint smile. "Did you think I wear a business suit twenty-four hours a day?"

"Maybe," he said easily. "I'm not going to apologize for coming to see you without an invitation or advance notice." His glance shifted to the streak of mud across her cheek, then he brought his gaze back to hers. "I suppose I could have chosen a better time."

Emma didn't bother with any attempt to make herself more presentable. Anything short of a shower and clean clothes would be wasted effort anyway.

"Did I leave something out of the Milligan file?" she asked.

"I don't know. I haven't read it."

Now she really was confused. "You told me this morning that it was important for me to finish the research for the Milligan case by five tonight so you could look through it before the hearing tomorrow."

"It's still on Linda's desk. I had more important things on my mind, like my paralegal walking out on me."

"Now it's the water-dripping-on-a-stone technique," she murmured. "You're not going to wear me down, Mr. Knight. I'm not coming back to Kimball and Knight."

Walking toward her, Turner gave her a crooked smile. "The least you can do for the man who has been assaulted by your vicious guard dog is to use his first name."

She glanced at the smears of mud below his knees. "Dragon has never mastered the fine art of shaking hands."

"Dragon?" Turner looked down at the gray-and-white dog. "Evidently I'm not as well read as I thought. I had the impression dragons were gigantic green monsters with scales who breathed fire and chased after fair damsels."

"The Shih Tzu breed is known as the lion dog of Tibet. She looks more like the south end of a dust mop than a lion, but she was practically breathing fire when a friend found her in a Dumpster where she'd been discarded as a puppy."

"A female dragon?"

"There had to be little dragons to grow up into big dragons."

"Of course," he said. "I don't know how that could have slipped my mind."

Emma shrugged her slender shoulders. "It seemed appropriate at the time."

"As long as she doesn't actually breathe fire, we'll get along just fine."

This wasn't even close to the reception he'd expected when he came to see her, but Turner had no complaints. Emma was talking to him naturally for the first time with only a faint reserve in her eyes, and he was fascinated. It was as though she had shed her distant manner when she'd removed her business attire.

The professional Emma had attracted him. This woman made his mouth go dry. He'd never craved a woman before, not like this. His desire was a grinding hunger to possess and be possessed, to give and take, to release the need coiled too tightly for too long.

Emma managed to take his mind off that need by bluntly asking, "Why are you here?"

"I would have thought that was obvious. I want to talk to you."

She reached down to pick up the hose, twisting the nozzle to shut off the spray of water. "What about?"

"That's the first dumb thing I've ever heard you say," he murmured. When he noticed she was planning to coil the hose and put it away, he took hold of it. She resisted, and he tugged harder. She tightened her grip and took a step back, stumbling when Dragon got in her way.

Turner reached out to catch her, his arm snaking around her waist and inadvertently bringing her close to his body for balance.

For a moment the dog, the hose, the world disappeared as he looked into her fathomless eyes. Her moist mouth was only inches away from his, her breasts pressed against his chest. He could feel the dampness of her jeans through the material covering his thighs, and her slender hips fit against his hard body perfectly.

Without releasing his hold on her, he shut his eyes and took a deep ragged breath until he won the battle for control. Barely. She felt so good. He wasn't sure he could let her go.

It didn't help when he felt her tremble in his arms.

Or when he heard the husky desperation in her voice as she told him to release her.

"I don't think I can," he admitted.

"You have to."

He loosened his arms enough so he could look down into her face. "Why? When it feels this good?"

Emma met his gaze. Her humiliation came flooding back, mixing in with anger that he would use his knowledge of her attraction to him to persuade her to do as he wanted.

"You've managed for two years without any trouble," she said harshly. "If you're trying to convince me you suddenly realized you're aware of me other than as a piece of efficient office equipment, don't bother. I won't believe it. I've never seen you use this tactic before, Knight, but coming on to me won't work either."

Turner dropped his arms and stepped back. This was the second time that he could have cheerfully throttled a woman. The same woman both times. Even his sister in her younger days as the world's most persistent pest had never made him as angry as Emma did.

"That was chemistry, Valerian. Not a macho attempt to seduce you into retracting your resignation. Since I'm evidently the only one affected, I'll try to keep my hands to myself."

Desperately needing something to occupy those hands, he bent down and picked up the hose. He took his time coiling the length into a large circle, every ounce of concentration on the task as though his life depended on doing it correctly.

When he finished, he asked roughly, "Where do you want this?"

"In the garage." She gathered up her trowel and the empty plant containers, then, with Dragon at her heels, led the way to the side door of the garage. Turner followed a few steps behind. Her car, an inexpensive white compact, was parked inside, but there was plenty of room to walk around it. Peg-Board lined the far wall with metal hooks attached to it holding various tools. He noted the number, making him again wonder if a man lived with her.

His sister, Silver, would consider his reasoning highly sexist, but Turner didn't know any women who knew a ratchet screwdriver from a soldering iron, much less owned either one. Both were hanging above a scarred wooden workbench that had obviously been used many times.

"Did all these tools come with the house?" he asked.

She was obviously puzzled by the question. "No. I bought them. The house was what the realtor called a 'fixer-upper.' I learned what that meant after I moved in. I still have a few projects left on the list of things that need to be done."

"You did the repairs yourself?"

"With the help of instruction books."

He shouldn't have been surprised. He'd seen the results when she applied her persistence and intelligence to a problem. Repairing plumbing would be a piece of cake for her.

Lifting the hose, he asked again, "Where do you want this?"

Pointing, Emma silently indicated where the hose went, then put her gardening equipment away. When she had nothing else to occupy herself, she turned to ask him to leave. She saw him looking down at his hands, then glancing around her workshop. She guessed he was looking for something to wipe the mud off his hands. She didn't need one of her etiquette manuals to inform her that she should offer him a place to wash. After all, it had been her dirt, her hose, and her dog responsible for the condition of his hands and jeans.

Her teeth worried her bottom lip as she thought about her options. There weren't very many. She could suggest he rinse off his hands under the outdoor faucet, or she could get a pail of water, soap, and a towel from the kitchen and bring them out to him. Or she could allow him inside her house.

Turner watched the emotions pass over Emma's face and waited. He not only could read each expression, but he also had a fair idea what she was thinking. That was a minor miracle, considering he'd never mastered the ability to do either one before. If he wasn't so fascinated by this new development, he might have wondered why Emma's feelings were suddenly so transparent to him.

He even knew the exact moment she came to a decision.

Turning toward the door, she said with little enthusiasm, "You can wash up in the kitchen before you leave."

Because her back was to him, Emma didn't see him smile, but she heard the dry amusement in his voice as he said, "Now that wasn't so hard, was it?"

He'd never know, she thought with resignation. No one but herself and Dragon had ever been in her house, except for an occasional visit from her neighbor, Audrey Twosteps. Sadie refused even to come for a visit.

No man had ever crossed her threshold, not even Audrey's husband, Dory. His job kept him on the road most of the time, and Emma tactfully limited her visits with Audrey when he was home. Any repair work that needed to be done, from wiring an outlet for a ceiling fan to fixing a leaking faucet, she did herself. It wasn't that she was too cheap to pay someone else to do the work. Her childhood had made her extremely independent and self-sufficient. She had learned early to rely only on herself, and it hadn't ever occurred to her to hire anyone to do the repairs.

Now she'd invited Turner into her home, the one man who'd ever made her think there was something missing in her life.

And the last man who would fill the emptiness.

Three

Dragon bounded into the house the second Emma opened the back door. The water dish was her destination, and her claws made tiny taps as she crossed the red-brick-tiled floor of the kitchen. It was the only sound in the room, since neither Emma nor Turner bothered to make polite conversation as they stepped into the kitchen.

Emma took a clean towel from a drawer and handed it to Turner. Indicating the sink with a wave of her hand, she said, "There's a bar of soap next to the faucets."

Without waiting to see if he took the hint, she stepped into a room off the kitchen. Turner caught a glimpse of a white washer and dryer against the far wall of the small utility room before she shut the door. He had gotten the worst mud off his jeans and was washing his hands when she returned wearing a blue denim work shirt instead of the soaked T-shirt. She still wore the jeans, which hadn't gotten as wet as the shirt. She had also tied back her hair with a red bandanna, but several strands rebelled confinement and brushed against her cheek.

He didn't comment on her change of clothing. Part of him was relieved. Temptation had never been so difficult to resist as the sight of Emma's taut nipples pressed against that wet white cloth. Although it was a shame to cover such a delectable part of her anatomy.

Rinsing his hands under the stream of water, he glanced at her again over his shoulder. She was standing as though poised for flight. If she stood any stiffer, he thought, her spine would be in danger of snapping.

"There's enough water for two," he invited.

"I'll wait until you're through."

Several drops of water fell from his hand to the floor when he reached out and grasped her wrist. Drawing her over to the sink to stand beside him, he asked, "Haven't you heard of conserving water?"

Sliding his arm under hers, he stuck her hands under the water and worked the soap into a lather. He could almost feel the battle she was waging inside as he ran his soapy hands over hers. He also knew the exact moment she decided to give in rather than fight.

With Emma, he was discovering slow progress was better than no progress at all. Usually he became impatient when he had to wait for something he wanted. With Emma, he was finding the anticipation was as intriguing as she was.

She took the soap from him and proceeded to scrub her soiled hands thoroughly without his help. The triumph he felt when she didn't move away was ridiculous considering it was such a small matter. He had to wonder how he was going to react when he touched her in a more intimate way. If it was anything like the sensations he was getting from just standing close to her, he was liable to explode.

Her thigh brushed against his when she silently offered the soap back to him. He almost dropped the slippery bar as desire speared through him, making him wish the water was ice cold instead of warm.

He stepped to one side to put a little distance between them and picked up the towel she'd given him earlier. Any other time, any other woman, and he would have dismissed the casual touch as an innocent accident.

With Emma, he couldn't think of the slightest physical contact ever being either casual or innocent.

Common sense made him stand back mentally and physically, giving himself time to cool down. In his office, he had finally admitted the physical attraction wasn't going to go away on its own. That was why he was there.

He just hoped he could slow down enough to give her time to catch up to what he wanted and to persuade her she wanted him too. First, he had to change her mind about disliking him.

As he dried his hands he looked around her kitchen, trying to get his mind off the arousal tightening his body. The room was as much of a surprise as her changed appearance had been. The table, chairs, and cupboards were painted a warm blue, the curtains a soft yellow, reminding him of a summer day full of sunshine and blue skies. Several green leafy plants were sitting on the windowsill over the sink.

The ivy she'd had on her desk for the last year was sitting in the center of the table. The appliances, countertop, and floor were spotlessly clean. Several decorative wooden shelves were hung at intervals on one wall with an assortment of cookbooks on each one, along with baskets and small pieces of pottery. Bookmarks stuck out of several of the cookbooks, and some of the bindings were worn and faded. Embroidered framed samplers and copper and ceramic molds were scattered in an attractive display on another wall. The combination of colors and decorations created an oddly soothing and cozy atmosphere, although if he was asked, Turner wouldn't have been able to explain why he thought so.

The kitchen in his apartment was always immaculate and orderly, too, thanks to a fanatical cleaning service. Except for the addition of a coffeepot on the counter, it looked pretty much as it had the day he moved in. His main requirement in his apartment had been its location, not whether or not it was decorated in any particular way. He used his place as somewhere to store his clothes, shave, shower, and sleep. Emma obviously cared how her home looked and had spent a great deal of time and thought on her surroundings.

Aware that she was looking at him, he met her solemn gaze and handed her the towel. "I was just admiring your kitchen. It's charming."

"Thank you."

"How long have you lived here?"

After a short pause she answered, "Almost two years. I bought the house three months after coming to work for Kimball and Knight."

He knew it would be worth his life to smile at the reluctance in her voice. She hadn't wanted to give him even that small bit of information, but she had. She was altogether too good at hiding her feelings, and he again wondered why she felt it was necessary.

The empty pages in the book entitled *Emma Valerian* had fewer blank areas since he'd arrived at her home, and he was more determined than ever to have every single page open to him.

Maybe if he was more open with her, she would get the hang of it.

Leaning against the counter, he said casually, "I took over the lease on a friend's apartment when he patched up the cracks in his marriage and went back to his wife and children. I didn't want to take the time to look for furnishings and offered to buy whatever furniture Bill didn't want. Aside from the bed, which I replaced, the apartment looks pretty much like it did the day I moved in."

"Considering the hours you put in at the office, I don't imagine you spend much time there anyway."

"True," he agreed. "Seeing the way you've decorated this room has made me realize how much I hate the color of the walls in my place."

"What color are they?"

"Green," he said, as though the word left a bad taste in his mouth. "Not grass green or emerald green, but the color of guacamole dip gone bad. Come to think of it, the furniture and the carpet in the living room are the same color."

She gave him a puzzled look. "How long have you lived there?"

He shrugged. "Three years, give or take a few months."

Her eyes widened. "If you don't like it, why haven't you changed it?"

"To what?"

"To whatever you like. You live there." She tilted her head to one side and gave him an assessing glance. "I know what your problem is. You would feel more at home if you had Mrs. Kimball come in to decorate your apartment so it would look like your office. Then you'd feel right at home."

It required a great deal of effort for Turner not to gape at her. Her eyes were glittering with amusement, her head tilted slightly, and that damn Mona Lisa smile was curving her soft mouth.

She was teasing him!

"Cute, Valerian. Real cute," he said, keeping his response light. "I'm beginning to get a complex. That's the third time today I've been reminded I spend too much time at the office."

"Maybe that's because you do. There are other things in life than work."

"So I've heard." She hadn't asked him the question, but he wanted the answer to it from her. "Do you live alone?"

Her gaze went to the little dog, who was amusing herself with a rawhide bone. "Not exactly."

Turner heard the hesitation in her voice again. She wasn't comfortable talking about herself. She was just going to have to get used to it, he decided.

"No man around to clutter up the place?"

"No."

"Not ever or not at the moment?"

Turner could give Dragon lessons in persistence,

Emma thought. It wasn't the first time she had witnessed Turner's unrelenting quest for facts, but it was the first time the subject had been her personal life.

"Both," she replied, saving evasions for when they might be necessary.

Turner nodded as she confirmed what he'd suspected, and he was irrationally pleased there hadn't been another man there before him.

It was surprisingly easy to imagine sitting down at her table with a cup of coffee and the morning paper, Emma sitting across from him. Her hair would be mussed from his fingers, and she would be wearing one of his shirts. And nothing else. Her dark eyes would be soft with satisfaction, her lips moist and slightly swollen from contact with his.

Turner mentally shook himself, suppressing the tantalizing images. His mouth twisted in a wry grimace. It was easier for his mind to make that decision than his body. But he was going to have to work on it. Domestic scenes weren't something he opted for. In fact, he usually ran the other way when a woman even hinted she was interested in more than a fleeting association. He always made it clear he wasn't the pipe-and-slippers type.

From the looks of her kitchen, Emma was more domesticated than most of the career women he knew. He should be running like hell in the opposite direction.

"I like what I've seen of your place so far," he said. He glanced at the door leading from the kitchen as a silent hint to be invited to see more.

He could tell by the way she bit her lip again that she was struggling with the decision to show him the rest of her home. Discovering this unsure side of his paralegal was as startling as her altered appearance.

"I promise," he murmured, "not to pry into the closets or peek under your bed."

She didn't respond to the teasing tone in his voice. Gazing at him with a serious expression, she said, "I wish I knew why you were really here."

"I realized you were right," he answered. "I don't know you, not the real Emma who owns a dog and plants flowers. I'm going to change that. In the process, you'll get to know me."

The sun had almost disappeared over the horizon, filling the room with deepening shadows. As if she needed to dispel any sense of intimacy, Emma walked over to the light switch and flicked it on.

"I've worked for you for two years," she said, "and you haven't shown any curiosity about where I live, or wanting to get to know me. Why now?"

"I have a policy about not getting personally involved with the people who work for me."

Her eyes met his with their usual somber expression. "Because we don't have a working relationship any longer, you feel free to come to my house in order to get to know me better? I don't think so. You're here to try to talk me into coming back to work. You've already admitted that, Turner."

She'd used his name. Such a small thing, he thought with amazement as a satisfying warmth flowed through him. Yet such a major thing with Emma. It had only taken two years. He wasn't going to wait that long for the next step in their relationship. He couldn't even guarantee he'd be able to wait for her to adjust to the change.

"I'm not letting you go out of my life without a fight."

"Are you suggesting we become personally involved?"

"You've always been good at grasping things quickly."

"That's part of the problem. This is too sudden."

He shook his head. "You've been under my skin for two long years."

Emma stared at him, seeing the truth in his eyes. As badly as she would have liked to believe he was serious, she had to remember why they couldn't go any further.

"We can't get involved," she said flatly.

"Why not?"

"I have my reasons."

"Maybe I'd believe you if you tell me what they are." His glance shifted to the table and chairs. "We can talk here or I can take you out to dinner if you would feel more comfortable in neutral territory. I don't care where as long as we clear up a few things."

Compromise had never been easy for her. Emma was more comfortable with black or white than gray. But how did a person stop a steamroller once he had a full head of steam? she wondered. She'd always admired Turner's relentless pursuit of right over wrong, fact over fiction, truth over lies. For some reason he was directing that same pursuit toward her.

She couldn't let him change her mind. If she spent more time with him, she was afraid he'd somehow do exactly that. "There's nothing to clear up. I've given my notice, and for some reason you're being stubborn about accepting it. That's not my problem. I'd like you to leave. I have things to do."

The step she took toward the door brought her near him. He reached out to cup the back of her neck, effectively stopping her from going any farther. She looked at him, eyes wide with surprise, but without fear.

"I'm going to make you change your mind about me, Emma," he warned softly. "And it has nothing to do with whether or not you come back to Kimball and Knight."

Her pride wouldn't let her evade the issue. Anger replaced her earlier humiliation. In the past, she'd seen examples of his arrogance, but tonight he had surpassed himself. Where did he get off telling her how she should feel or not feel? she thought as she glared at him.

"What difference could it possibly make to you how I feel, Mr. Knight?" she asked frostily. "My feelings are my business, not yours."

She fired off Turner's temper by returning to the formal use of his name. To give himself time to cool down, he took the towel she'd discarded on the counter and gently scrubbed a streak of mud on her cheek with a damp corner.

She was apparently so surprised by his actions, she didn't move.

Holding her gaze with his, Turner thought he detected more than surprise in the depths of her eyes. He finally recognized the expression. Desire. Did that mean she didn't dislike him after all? That she was attracted to him? Stunned, he wondered if he'd misread her feelings for the last two years.

He was going to find out, he decided, but as he

lowered his head to taste her parted lips, he was jolted by a sudden stab of pain in his stomach.

The burning sensation returned in full force, and he flinched when it curled into a searing agony, stronger than anything he'd ever felt before. He pressed the palm of his hand over the area where the pain was the worst.

Emma placed her own hand on his arm. "It's back, isn't it?"

"It's nothing." Taking a deep breath after the sharp twinge eased, he returned to the original subject. "As a rule, lawyers aren't overly sensitive about people disliking them. I don't know too many of my fellow legal eagles who would win popularity contests with their adversaries any more than I would. I usually don't give a damn if I'm considered a nice guy or not, but I find I do care about your opinion of me. I'll be damned if I know why, but I do. Now, I admit I can occasionally be a demanding pain in the butt sometimes. . . ."

He found himself smiling when her reaction to his last statement was a raised brow.

"All right, a large pain in the butt. If you come back, I can't guarantee I won't be just as much of a slave driver as before."

Emma was more concerned about the pain he'd obviously felt a minute ago. It would do wonders for her ego if she could believe that flare of pain was caused by concern over her opinion of him, but she knew there was a more reasonable explanation. On several occasions in the last couple of weeks, she'd seen him wince, press his hand against his stomach, and reach for his antacids. She'd even overheard Harry telling Turner he was a prime candidate for an ulcer from the stress he was putting himself under and the long hours he put in. It was as good an explanation as any as to what might be wrong with him.

Then something else he'd said occurred to her. *Lawyers aren't overly sensitive about people disliking them.* Turner had misunderstood her feelings toward him. He thought she didn't like him!

Relief washed over her. Since he'd given her back her pride, she could afford to ease his. "I don't know why it matters to you, but I have my own reasons for not being very friendly at work. Like you, I've discovered it's better not to mix business with pleasure." She patted his arm in a placating gesture, then stepped back, dropping her hands at her sides. "Now, will that satisfy you?"

Turner brought his hand up to his arm, where she had touched him. Damned if he couldn't feel the imprint of each finger as though they'd seared his skin through his shirt.

He smiled faintly. "I'm not even close to being satisfied. I still want to know why you're so intent on quitting your job. If it isn't because you're fed up with me and my demanding ways, why can't you stay with us?"

She shook her head in bemusement. "You're not going to give up, are you?"

"You've known me for two years, Emma. What do you think?"

"I think you're not going to give up."

Perspiration broke out on his forehead as he fought the wrenching pain, which struck again with relentless fury. "You're right, but I'm going to back off. At least for tonight." He took two steps toward her back door, then stopped to glance at her. "Will you at least work out your two weeks?"

Maybe if she hadn't seen the sweat break out on his unusually pale skin or the way he was holding his side, she would have stood her ground. Instead she caved in. "I'll be at work tomorrow. I won't promise more than that."

"Good," was his only comment, and it came out more like a grunt. Then he was gone as suddenly as he had arrived.

Dragon followed Emma to the front window in the living room. She didn't try to pretend she wasn't watching Turner leave. He would be able to see her standing at the window if he glanced toward the house. He didn't look back once.

She could almost feel the effort he was putting into each step he took toward his car parked at the curb. When he finally managed to slide into the driver's seat, he didn't start the engine right away. Instead he leaned forward to rest his forehead on his hands, which were gripping the top of the steering wheel.

Emma couldn't stand seeing him like this. She had started toward the front door when she heard the engine turn over. Returning to the window, she watched him drive away. Then she walked over to the bookshelf on the opposite side of the living room, where she removed a copy of *Gray's Anatomy* and several medical textbooks.

Settling into her favorite chair, she spent the next thirty minutes reading up on the symptoms and treatment of ulcers and making notes. Her research bore out her suspicions. The symptoms she'd witnessed were listed. Turner needed to be examined by a doctor and get medication. Pain was a warning he was ignoring.

When Dragon plopped down at her feet, Emma bent over and smoothed her hand over the Shih Tzu's long hair. "Maybe you have the right idea, Dragon. You wear down resistance by persistence in order to get your way. I could try that on Turner the next time he has one of those attacks. And if nagging doesn't work, I'll call the paramedics to come and drag him off to the hospital."

Turner would hate her interference, but she hated seeing him in pain. If he didn't have an ulcer, he had something similar. Whatever it was wasn't going to go away on its own.

She put her hand under the dog's jaw to raise Dragon's head. "It looks like I'm not going to be home tomorrow after all, Dragon."

With that thought, Emma stepped over the dog and replaced the medical textbooks on the shelves. Glancing at her watch, she saw it was only eight o'clock. There were a number of things she could do until it was time for bed. She could fix herself something to eat, work up in her studio, take Dragon for a long walk.

Instead she returned to the chair and sat there for over an hour. At one point she almost rose to put on a sweater against the chill, but she realized the cold was from inside her. She knew the difference, having been chilled to the bone too many times to count. Remembering how difficult her life had once been made her think about Sadie and wonder if the older woman's cough was any better.

Emma knew she should go see Sadie that night.

It had been almost a week since her latest argument with the stubborn woman who'd been her guide, her friend, her salvation, at a time when Emma had desperately needed all three.

Because she was so familiar with the life, she hated the thought of Sadie living on the streets. Now that Emma had a home, she couldn't see why Sadie kept refusing to live with her. Once neither of them had had a choice about their hand-to-mouth existence, but things were different now, better, safer. Still, Sadie wouldn't leave the streets and the people she felt needed her there.

No, Emma decided. She wouldn't go looking for Sadie that night. She was still too angry that the older woman wouldn't let her take care of her now that she could.

She left the chair to get Dragon's leash. As she walked the dog in the quiet neighborhood, she had company other than Dragon—a haunting loneliness she hadn't felt for a long time.

Four

Emma arrived at the office of Knight and Kimball at her regular time. Aside from a couple of curious glances from Turner's secretary, everything was the same as usual. The phones rang, clients kept appointments to see Turner or to sign papers. Harry phoned from New York to check that the office was still chugging along and reassured Turner that he would be returning on Monday with stacks of photographs and videos of his new granddaughter.

The deliveryman from the office-supply store screwed up the order between their office and a pediatrician named Kincaid.

"Maybe we should have kept the case of lollipops to sweeten Turner's mood," Harry's secretary remarked as she paused to pick up the mail Linda had sorted.

Turner's secretary was pleased to announce that Turner had come in whistling under his breath that morning, something he hadn't done in months. His mood seemed sweet enough, for a change.

Emma found that wasn't quite the truth, but close enough. At least Turner hadn't appeared smug about persuading her to return when she answered his first summons of the morning. From then on her workday continued pretty much the way it always had.

Only one small incident had been out of the ordinary. When she first sat down at her desk, she spotted a piece of paper, folded and partially tucked under the blotter on her otherwise empty desk. A note had been scrawled on it. *I find this in Mr. T's trash.* It was signed *Maria.*

Puzzled, Emma picked up the paper. It was wrinkled, as though it had been crumpled and then smoothed out. Why would the woman who cleaned the office at night leave her a scrap of paper Turner had thrown away? she wondered. Maria occasionally left cookies for her to show her appreciation for Emma getting her the job so she no longer had to sleep on the streets, but this was different.

Unfolding it, Emma sucked in her breath as she recognized the image that had been expertly sketched. By Turner? she wondered, searching for an explanation why her likeness had been drawn so beautifully, then discarded. And why he'd felt compelled to draw her at all.

The drawing wasn't a case of Turner idly doodling while engrossed in a phone call. The hand that had sketched her portrait was exceptionally talented in a way she would never be.

Emma carefully refolded the paper and tucked it into her purse.

A little after four that afternoon, she was on her way to the record room and Turner was standing in the hall, waiting with a client for one of the elevators to arrive. She saw him frown at the tall stack of clients' records she was balancing precariously in her arms.

"Emma, for crying out loud," he said crossly. "What are you doing?"

She gave him a glance that indicated he'd just asked a particularly stupid question, but since a client was standing nearby, she refrained from saying so.

"You specifically asked that these records be filed today."

For a long moment he simply looked at her, his expression unreadable, until the elevator pinged its arrival. "Next time take a cart, or ask someone to help you, or make more than one trip."

"Yes, sir," she said obediently.

He ushered the client into the elevator, but instead of following the gentleman, he placed his hand on the edge of the door to keep it from closing.

"Ask me to dinner tonight," he ordered quietly.

"Why?" she whispered.

"I'm coming over to your house, and it would be rude of me to arrive for dinner unless I was asked, so invite me."

The elevator door was clunking back and forth in protest and the client wasn't looking too happy about the delay. Turner never took his gaze from her face and looked set to stay there as long as necessary to get the answer he wanted.

Emma felt the stack of folders begin to slide to the left. Shifting her balance, she said quickly, "Seven o'clock. Potluck. Don't be late."

It wasn't the most gracious invitation he'd ever had, but Turner accepted it with a quick nod of his head, then stepped into the elevator. It really wouldn't do to turn cartwheels in front of a client as stuffy as Gustave Aldershot, he thought, or to kiss the top of his bald little head. Turner felt like doing both. He had to settle for crossing his arms over his chest and leaning against the back of the elevator while he thought about the evening with a great deal of pleasure and anticipation.

A few hours later some of the delight and self-satisfaction dimmed as he sat down at the table in Emma's kitchen. It wasn't due to being disappointed in Emma in any way. She'd met him at the door wearing white jeans, a burnt-orange cotton sweater, and a wary expression, which he'd expected.

Dinner was only an excuse he'd used to get himself invited to her house, but she had taken it seriously. The table in the kitchen had been set for two, and she'd even sprung for a bottle of wine.

Turner peered into the casserole dish she'd placed on the table between them. At first he thought this was the first course. He was wrong. The casserole plus a tossed salad was the meal.

After she served a generous helping of something green covered with golden cheese onto his plate, he stabbed at it with his fork. "It's colorful and smells good. Would I be rude if I asked what is it?"

"Broccoli casserole," Emma said, biting back a smile at the tentative way he was poking his food, as though there was a possibility it would poke back.

"I did say it would be potluck," she added. "Remember? This is what I planned to have for dinner."

"Hmmm," he murmured. "Do you have anything against red meat?"

"Nothing personal," she said, shrugging. "I just don't eat it."

He raised his eyes to meet hers, his expression mildly horrified. "Never?"

"I tried to eat a hamburger once when I was into rebelling against everything I'd been taught as a child. I didn't get past the first bite."

"Your parents are vegetarians?"

"The people I lived with prefer to call themselves naturalists. They consider it against nature to eat flesh of our fellow creatures on earth." She chuckled. "You should see your face. You look as though I was talking about people from outer space. I would think you of all people would be accustomed to people who live alternative life-styles."

"Why me of all people?"

"Shortly after I came to work for Kimball and Knight, there was an article in one of the news magazines about your father receiving some kind of award from the Queen of England. The article covered how he gave up the department-store chain that had been in the Knight family for aeons to go to England and devote himself to his work as an equine artist. And this at a time in his life when most men his age would be thinking of doing nothing more challenging than improving their golf game. I got the impression King Knight marches to his own drummer. In their own way, the naturalists do too. Their drummer just happens to be a bit more bizarre than most people's."

"Your parents aren't living?"

She shrugged again. "I don't know. I haven't seen any of them for a number of years."

"How many parents did you have?"

She evaded his question by answering, "It's a little complicated."

Turner started eating the casserole as he thought about what she'd said. From her tone of voice he could practically see the Keep Out signs wrapped with barbed wire she'd erected. She'd apparently told him all she planned to about the people who'd raised her. It was a shame. They sounded like the type of people his father would find fascinating. Turner's curiosity was more basic. They were part of Emma, which made them of interest to him, another page in her life.

He looked up when Emma asked sweetly, "Would you like some more?"

Glancing down at his plate, he saw he'd eaten every bite. He shook his head. "It was good, but I don't think I should push my luck. My system is accustomed to steak."

"Maybe that's why you're having problems with your stomach."

He frowned at her, but she simply met his gaze and waited for his argument. He didn't give her one. Instead he said, "You still haven't given me a good explanation why you're so determined to leave Kimball and Knight."

Time to give in to his persistence, she thought. "Instead of trying to explain, it might save some time if I show you why."

Turner followed her when she walked out of the kitchen, puzzled over her choice of words.

His first impression of her living room was of books and more books covering one entire wall from floor to ceiling. Another wall had shelves stuffed with even more books, which stood on either side of a gas fireplace. A wooden rocking chair sat near the hearth. On the floor on one side was a stack of books, and a couple of books were on the small table on the other side. Aside from a couch that was little bigger than a love seat, there wasn't any other pieces of furniture on the polished wood floor. Floral upholstery, a checkered cushion on the rocking chair, a braided rug, and printed draperies shouldn't go together, but somehow they did. He knew even less about decorating styles than he did about Emma, but the room reminded him of something out of the decorating magazines Harry's wife was always browsing through. Like the photo layouts in those magazines, there was no television set or evidence that someone actually lived in the room, aside from the bookmarks sticking out of the books.

"I guess you're not a sports fan," he said.

She gave him a blank look. "Why would you think I would be?"

"Wishful thinking. Sports are about all I watch on television, when a team I like is playing and I have the time. I notice you don't have a set, so I assume you spend your evenings with all these books rather than watching television."

"I never got into the habit of watching television. There weren't any where I grew up."

"Where did you grow up?" he asked casually as he stepped closer to the shelves to read some of the book titles. "In a foreign country?"

"Close enough."

Turner ran a finger over the spines of the books at his eye level, amazed at the variety of titles. A book of etiquette was next to a manual on plumbing repairs. Law books and current best-sellers vied for space with gardening and how-to-fix-just-about-anything books.

He turned to comment on the assortment of subjects and saw Emma wasn't lingering in the living room. She was walking toward the stairs, which he presumed led to the bedrooms. His body was more than willing to carry out any plans she might have in her bedroom, but his common sense told him he was indulging in wishful thinking. Whatever she was going to show him, it had nothing to do with lovemaking.

After reaching the landing, she passed a partially opened door and entered the room next to it. As he followed he caught a glimpse in the first room of a wide brass bed covered with a navy-blue-and-gold bedspread made out of some sort of shiny material. Promising himself he'd see the inside of her bedroom another time made it easier for him to walk by.

The room Emma had entered was a bedroom that had been turned into a workroom. A drafting table was under a length of fluorescent lighting. A tabouret holding drawing supplies was parked next to a high stool. One shelf unit held neatly stacked pads of drawing paper. Another held rows of slim books. A desk with a computer sat on the other side of the room, away from the wide, curtainless window.

Considering he was the son of an artist and had been exposed to artwork for most of his life, Turner's question was incredibly stupid. That didn't stop him from asking it.

"What's all this?"

Emma walked over to the desk and lifted a folder. She handed it to him. "This is a dummy of a children's book I've had accepted by a publisher."

Dummy was a good word to describe how he felt. Slowly, carefully, he turned several pages. The illustrations had been done in gouache, an opaque watercolor, and the drawings were charming and whimsical. The story was about a young turtle who wanted to venture out on her own and met a number of obstacles along her way, proving she hadn't been as ready as she thought to be independent. Turner became caught up in the tale, turning one page after the other until he reached the end.

Finally, he closed the mock-up book. When he glanced up to look at Emma, he realized she had been nervously waiting for him to finish reading her story. She was worrying her bottom lip with her teeth again. He was irrationally pleased that she was anxious about his opinion.

"My experience with children's books is limited, Emma, but this is a terrific story. I couldn't put it down once I started reading it. I was rooting for Chigger from page one."

Emma's relief was as obvious as her earlier nervousness had been. She smiled, the first genuine smile she'd ever given him, and he had to tighten his hold on his control to stop from tasting the smile on her tempting mouth.

"You should do that more often," he said softly.

"I am. I started another children's book when I finished *Chigger*."

He shook his head. "I mean you should smile more often. Why haven't you ever smiled at the office? The other members of the staff do on occasion. They've even been known to laugh at Harry's corny jokes, so we can't be that miserable to work for. You have a lovely smile, Emma. It's a shame to keep it all to yourself."

She took the book from him and made a big deal out of putting it back on the desk, her smile gone as quickly as it had come.

It took only two steps for him to close the distance between them. With his fingers under her chin, he made her look at him. "You've let me into your house and shown me your work, Emma. You've trusted me that far. I'm going to push my luck and ask you why you were so unapproachable at the office."

She met his gaze. "I didn't want to lose my job."

Even though she hadn't said it, Turner guessed, "Again?"

She stepped to the side, and he dropped his hand. This time her smile was faint with a hint of rueful amusement. "I've always admired your ability to read between the lines when it came to dealing with clients and witnesses. It's a little disconcerting to have that turned directly on me. You're right, of course. Before I came to Kimball and Knight, I worked for another legal firm, where a simple smile along with 'good morning' was treated as an invitation."

"Bender, Trent and Bender," he said. He'd reread her résumé before leaving the office that day. "Which one made the pass at you?"

"It doesn't matter."

"It matters, Emma," he said tightly, hating the thought of any man touching her. "I'll make a calculated guess and say it was Stuart Trent, since

I've seen him hit on every woman in a room as though he were sampling all the items on a buffet before deciding which one to devour."

By not denying what he said, Emma knew she'd silently given him his answer. "I left before things became impossible. It was a no-win situation. If I received a raise or a promotion, everyone would say it was because I was sleeping with one of the bosses. If I didn't, they would say I either wouldn't put out or wasn't very good. I decided the advice in a book I'd read on office procedures was right. To be treated as a professional, one must look and act like a professional."

That explained why she hadn't been very friendly in the office, but not why she was leaving his law firm. "I haven't made a pass at you, and I seriously doubt if Harry has either, so why the resignation? You've evidently been working on your children's books in your spare time. I'm sure Harry would agree if you worked only a couple of days a week for us and took the rest of the time for your writing. You need money to live on, and you said the pay you received at Kimball and Knight was more than adequate. I meant what I said about us needing you right now, Emma. Couldn't we work something out?"

Since she couldn't very well tell him she was resigning partly because she was so strongly attracted to him, she settled for what she could admit. "I like my job at Kimball and Knight, but I can't go any further there. I've been taking a few courses at San Jose State in the evening to get a degree in graphic art. The next class will start up again the first week in April."

"You're taking art classes?"

She nodded and waited for him to make a comment. He looked at her for a full minute but didn't say another word.

"I've researched the children's-book market," she went on, "and realize I won't make enough to live on even if I'm lucky enough to get more books published. With the advances from the books and selling designs for greeting cards, I can make a little extra money for art supplies. I've paid my mortgage for a year and have enough money saved to keep me in peanut butter and dog food."

Turner walked over to the drawing board and looked down at the sketch she'd been working on. A pencil was resting on the sheet of paper, and he picked it up.

Turning the pencil over and over, he said, "It's not going to be easy to make a living as an artist. There's a lot of competition out there."

Emma had never heard that particular defeated tone in his voice before. "Sometimes easy isn't always better. Haven't you ever wanted something that wasn't practical, something that didn't make any sense to other people but was vitally important to you?"

His answer was short, blunt, and bitter. "No."

She was long past the stage of caring whether anyone approved of what she did with her life. "Lucky you," she said dryly. "I'd rather shoot for the moon than stare at it from the ground."

"Even if there are other people better qualified to shoot for the same moon?"

What an odd conversation to be having, she thought. "It might be the same moon we'd be aiming for, but what I would do when I got to my goal would be different from anyone else. Maybe not better or worse, but mine."

"And that will be enough for you?"

"I hope so," she answered with a touch of humor. "It's something I have to do, something I need to try, to express myself in my own unique style. I might as well enjoy the trip."

Stepping closer, she noticed Turner wasn't holding the pencil in the way most people would, but with two fingers on top and the thumb underneath, as an experienced artist would. Thinking of the sketch the cleaning woman had left on her desk, she no longer questioned whether or not Turner had drawn it. She couldn't help wondering if he did something with his extraordinary talent, although with the hours he put in at the office, she couldn't imagine when he would find the time.

Standing beside him, she raised her gaze to his face and was startled by the look of longing in his eyes as he stared at her work.

Five

Afterward Emma couldn't have said what made her do it. The part of her conscience that usually warned her to mind her own business apparently had taken a vacation.

She reached for another pencil and, with the sharpened end, pointed to the face of the small boy she'd depicted kneeling in the grass holding a frog in his open palm.

"I don't have many problems drawing animals," she said, "but I don't do as well with facial expressions of children. I can't seem to get the look on this little boy's face right. At this point in the story, he's supposed to be fascinated and a little frightened of the frog that followed him from the pond." She glanced up from the sketch to Turner. "As you can see from the drawing, I've made him look like he's sitting on the sharp end of a pin."

Turner smiled at her description, his gaze never leaving the sketch. "The expression in his eyes shows wide-eyed wonder, but it's the shape of his mouth that makes him look like he's about to cry."

Emma studied the boy's mouth, then looked

carefully at the expression in his eyes. She also saw how tightly Turner's fingers were gripping the pencil. Following her instincts, she said, "Show me what you mean."

He set down the pencil with an abrupt movement. "I'm a lawyer, not an artist."

Maybe if she hadn't detected the flatness in his voice or hadn't seen the sketch he'd done of her, she wouldn't have pushed so hard. "I could use an objective opinion. You took one look at the drawing and immediately saw what was wrong. Please, Turner," she said, picking up the pencil and extending it toward him. "You can't possibly do any worse than I've done. All I do is draw him over and over, and his little face keeps coming out looking like this."

Turner could have given himself a variety of reasons for doing as she asked, and they would all have been true. It was a way to keep her near him. Her arm was brushing his, and she was standing close enough for him to catch her scent; a mixture of sunshine, earth, and female, an enticing combination. Plus it was the first time she'd ever asked him for anything. They were all valid reasons. But the one that had him taking the pencil from her was that he was itching to redraw the child's mouth, to give the boy the expression he should have.

It required only a few strokes of the pencil to alter the child's expression completely. The changes were minimal, but made all the difference in the mood of the picture.

"That's it," she said softly. "That's the expression I've been trying to get."

Turner's smile was a mirror image of the one he'd given the child.

Emma stared down at the drawing, then at his hand still holding the pencil. She could take a hundred classes, read a thousand books, and never acquire the talent apparent in Turner's natural ability. And he didn't consider himself an artist.

What did that make her?

Dejected, she took a step back and slumped down onto the stool. "I guess I've just been kidding myself."

Surprised by her sudden dispirited tone of voice, Turner glanced over at her. "About what?"

"That I could do artwork. I've taken numerous night classes for years, read every book I could find on perspective, foreshortening, shading, color, every aspect of drawing and painting. I've been struggling with that drawing for over a week, and a lawyer took one look at it and corrected it with only a couple of strokes of a pencil."

"You're being a little hard on yourself, Emma. I was taught to look at the world through the eyes of an artist for as long as I can remember. Most children learn their colors as red, blue, and yellow. In our case, a blue sky was cerulean with a touch of ultramarine blue and white. King wanted us to see with what he called the 'heart's eye' as well as our normal eyesight, to see the shape and feel the emotion in the smallest detail."

"Something I could never get out of books," she murmured. "If I had even half the talent you have, I would want to be an artist." With the ghost of a mocking laugh, she added, "I do have half the talent you have, and I think I can become an artist."

An all-too-familiar twist of pain caught Turner unaware, and he had to bite back a moan. A fine sheen of perspiration coated his skin, and he bent over the table as he fought the cruel timing of the insidious attack. The pencil in his fingers snapped in half with the force of his grip.

"Turner?" Emma's voice came through a haze of white-hot pain. "Turner, what's wrong?"

"Nothing," he growled, hating the weakness, hating Emma seeing him this way.

She obviously didn't believe him. "Don't tell me it's nothing. You're doubled over as though someone punched you, and you're suddenly as gray as a ghost."

"Gee, Emma," he drawled between quick gulps of air. "That makes me feel so much better."

"I've been trained as a paralegal, not as a diplomat."

He couldn't stop the groan that came out when she ran her hand over the front pocket of his jeans. "That's not helping."

"I'm looking for those antacids you eat like popcorn."

He didn't have time to wonder how she knew about the tablets. Now she was running her hand down the other pocket, and the moan escaping from him this time had nothing to do with the agony coiling inside his stomach.

"I didn't bring any antacids with me. Just give me a minute. It'll ease up."

When the minute passed and Turner was still hunched over with his arm curved around his middle, Emma took over. "I'm taking you to a doctor."

"Stop making such a big deal out of a little

stomachache. Something I had for lunch didn't agree with me, that's all. Maybe it was that broccoli whatever we had for dinner. No offense."

"You've had this before, so don't go blaming my broccoli casserole."

Sliding her arm around his waist, she started walking toward the door. "Dragon, get out of the way."

"Emma, calm down," Turner said.

Anger gave her the added strength she needed when he resisted. Half supporting him, she drew him with her to the landing. "You can kill yourself with stress at the office, in your car, or in the courtroom, but not in my house."

Even through the searing pain, he couldn't help but grin at her. "Throwing me out, Emma?"

"I should," she muttered, breathing more heavily as she assisted him to the stairs. "I really should. For the last couple of months you've been ignoring the signals your body has been trying to get through that thick skull of yours to tell you there is something wrong. Harry and your secretary have both tried to get you to slow down. But have you paid any attention? No, of course not. Not Turner Knight, Superman, able to take on more cases than ten men and leaping over the need for sleep or proper meals. Taking time off to relax is for mere mortals, not for the almighty Turner Knight."

If he'd felt better, Turner would have enjoyed her tirade, even though he usually hated anyone fussing over him. It was oddly soothing when Emma did it. Her ranting and raving made him realize something else. Emma genuinely cared about him.

He felt her arm tighten around his waist and

closed his eyes to savor the delicious feel of her hip rubbing against him.

In the next second he jerked his eyes open and glanced down to follow the path her hand was taking across the front of his jeans again. This time she slid her hand into the closest pocket. He could feel each finger wiggling and sliding over the thin lining of the pocket that separated her hand from his suddenly sensitive lower body.

Once again he groaned aloud as throbbing desire joined the burning ache in his stomach. "Good Lord, Emma. Just throw me down the stairs and get it over with instead of killing me slowly."

"I'm getting your car keys," she said crossly. "It would be easier if you didn't wear such tight jeans."

He was tempted to point out that the jeans hadn't fit so snugly until she started rummaging around in them.

"What are you going to do with my car keys?"

"Drive your car. What else?"

"I don't need you to drive me home, Emma. I can manage on my own."

"Good for you," she muttered, and kept delving into his pants until her fingers closed over the unmistakable shape of keys.

He tried being practical. That should appeal to her efficient little mind. "If you drive me to my place in my car, you won't have any way of getting home unless you drive mine back, which won't help me much in the morning when I need to get to the office." A solution occurred to him that had some merit. "Although you could come and pick me up in the morning. We could ride into the office in the morning, then I could bring you home."

"You're rambling on like a first-year lawyer arguing a losing case, counselor. Concentrate on putting one foot in front of the other instead. I can't get you to your car on my own."

The pain sharpened at the exact moment he was going to protest, leaving him little breath to argue with her. As soon as the burning let up, he would show her he was perfectly capable of driving his own car.

It took five minutes to get down the stairs and to his car parked in her driveway. At least Emma had the grace not to say "I told you so," he thought sourly as he leaned one arm on the roof of his Porsche while she unerringly found the correct key to unlock the door on the passenger side. For some reason, he couldn't come up with a single argument that was worth a damn, nor did he have the energy to fight Emma and the pain too.

"You'll need directions," he said, giving in as graciously as he could manage with a hot poker digging into his stomach.

She looked up. "Or I could just drive around all night."

Tilting his head to one side, he said, "I've known you for two years, and in all that time I never realized you had such a smart mouth."

She opened the car door. "I was sure I put that down on my résumé."

"In very small print apparently," he said as he shifted to slide into the car. "Get to East Santa Clara Street whichever route you want to take. I'll tell you where to turn off eventually."

"No problem," she said.

As Turner sank down onto the seat he closed his

eyes and took several shallow breaths. When he opened his eyes a few seconds later, Emma was seated behind the wheel and inserting the key into the ignition.

For a man who prided himself on being in control of every aspect of his life, he wondered why he wasn't resenting Emma taking over. And driving his car, for Pete's sake. The only other woman who'd ever driven his powerful car was his sister. Like Emma, she hadn't asked permission either.

"You'd get along great with Silver," he said.

"I'd get along with gold, too," she said wryly, "if I could ever afford any."

He smiled. "The Silver I'm talking about is my sister."

"Why do you think I would I get along with your sister?"

He closed his eyes and let his head drop back on the headrest. "You have a lot in common. You ignore any opposition or run right over it."

"I like her already." Downshifting as she stopped at a traffic light, she asked, "Is Silver really your sister's name or is it a nickname? Silver Knight sounds like someone out of a fairy tale."

"You're close. Her name is Silver Viviane Knight. My father wanted it the other way around with Viviane, the Lady of the Lake, as her first name, but according to my mother, he'd had his way giving us boys Arthurian names. She was putting her foot down when it came to saddling a girl with one as well."

"You mean Arthurian as in King Arthur and the Knights of the Round Table?"

"The very same."

"I hate to break this to you," she said as the light turned green and she pressed down on the accelerator, "but I've read a number of books about King Arthur and saw the movie *Camelot* twice. I don't remember any knight named Turner."

"Like my brothers, Michael and Ryder, I use my middle name."

The minute he said it, he knew he shouldn't have. One trait that made Emma a terrific paralegal was her curiosity and determination to find an answer she didn't know or facts to back up a supposition.

He felt oddly chagrined when she only nodded and said, "I understand perfectly. I haven't used my own first name since I was eleven."

Now he was the one intrigued. "Why? What is it?"

She flicked a glance in his direction. "Are you willing to tell me what yours is?"

He shook his head, stepping out of the trap he'd set himself. "You might run the car off the road while you're laughing hysterically."

"It's that bad?" she asked. "Your parents must be unusually devoted King Arthur fans if they chose names for their children from the legends."

Turner relaxed a little as the pain in his stomach lowered to a slow simmer. This bout had lasted longer than any others but was finally going away.

"My mother's ancestors lived in the southwest part of England, which includes Somerset County, where Avalon and Camelot were supposed to have been. Her family home is fairly near Glastonbury Abbey, where King Arthur and Queen Guinevere are allegedly buried. My mother was raised on tales of King Arthur and his gang and, in turn, told them to us."

"Your mother is English?"

"Was. She died four years ago."

"I'm sorry," she murmured.

"I am too," he said quietly. "She was a remarkable lady."

"In what way?"

Turner glanced at her profile, wishing he could see the expression in her eyes. The odd note in her voice, almost one of reverence, puzzled him. He'd heard that same tone in his grandmother's clipped English accent when she talked about "dear Sir Lancelot," who she insisted had been badly treated by Queen Guinevere.

When he didn't answer, Emma guessed her question must have been out of line. "I'm sorry. It was a rude question."

"I don't mind talking about her. I was trying to think of how to best describe Myra Knight. I could tell you what she looked like, but that would only give you a picture of her on the outside. It was what was inside her that made her special. She was very strict about manners and proper behavior, scolding us if we were rude to each other or didn't use the proper utensils at the table. Lord help us if we came to the table without being clean and properly dressed. Yet she would kneel for hours in wet sand to help us build a sandcastle on the beach. I remember her climbing up into the old tree in back of the house where Michael and I built a tree house, even though a herd of ladies were due to arrive for some committee meeting and she was wearing one of her best dresses."

Emma listened to every word. The woman he described with warmth and humor was as much a fantasy to her as the characters in the Arthurian legends.

"From what I've read about your father," she said, "he was born and raised in the United States. Did he become interested in the Knights of the Round Table because his last name was Knight or did he become involved after he married your mother?"

"His ancestors were also from England and brought their fascination with Camelot with them when they immigrated to this country. A number of our relatives feel the name Knight was handed down from one of the original knights who fought for King Arthur."

"Do you?"

"There could be worse things than having a knight or two in the family tree."

Emma had to agree with that, considering the many broken branches in her own family tree. She could imagine what Turner's reaction would be at the sparsity of her knowledge of her own ancestry. Or the fact that she had no idea what her legal last name was. The reactions of the few people she'd innocently told about her background when she was younger had been disbelief mixed with shock and topped off with distaste. Their response had been extreme enough to persuade her to keep her past to herself.

"In that article I read about your father," she went on, "there was something about a priceless chess set in King Knight's possession. Is that true?"

"One of our more dedicated ancestors, Willoughby Knight, spent his life sculpting a chess set featuring Arthurian figures made out of pure gold. He broke the molds after casting the pieces so there would only be one Camelot set in existence."

"So the Camelot chess set does exist?"

"It's in my father's possession in England."

Turner should have known better than to bring up the subject of the chess set and his father. Every time he thought about his father's summons, his stomach rebelled. This time was no exception.

Emma heard his breathing change. Turning onto East Santa Clara Street, she kept her attention on the road. The San Jose General Hospital was located off East Santa Clara, just ahead. She steeled herself for the upcoming battle with Turner. He wasn't going to like what she was about to do, and she couldn't really blame him. She knew he'd been under the impression she was taking him home. The fact that he hadn't put up more of a struggle about her driving had proved to her he was really in pain. And had been for quite some time, except he was too darn stubborn to admit it or do something about it.

No, he wasn't going to like stopping at the emergency room, but what could he do? she thought with amusement. Fire her?

"Why don't you let me in on the joke?"

She hadn't realized she'd chuckled aloud. The signs indicating how to get to the emergency room were clearly visible as she turned into the well-lighted parking area. Even if Turner was unfamiliar with the hospital, he only had to read the signs that seemed to be everywhere she looked.

"You might not think it's very funny," she said.

At that moment Turner saw one of the signs. "You'd better be here because you aren't feeling well, Emma," he said, his tone making her think of steel wrapped in velvet.

She pulled into the first available parking slot and shut off the engine. As she extinguished the headlights, she turned on the overhead interior light, taking all the time she could before she confronted him.

She met his furious glare with all the dread she would have been feeling if she were facing a firing squad.

"I was reading up on your symptoms last night in some medical textbooks, and they all point to the possibility that you have an ulcer. If you don't get it treated, it could get much worse and you might even have to have surgery. There are all sorts of complications, such as peritonitis and—"

"I don't have an ulcer," he said stubbornly, his hand unconsciously rubbing across his rib cage.

"Prove it," she challenged. "Go have some tests done and prove you don't have an ulcer."

She held her breath as she waited for the explosion of his temper. It never came. Instead Turner simply stared at her. His silence lasted for what seemed like hours, and she was beginning to feel very uncomfortable under his intense examination.

Finally he said, "All right."

It was her turn to stare. His compliance had come too easy. "You mean you'll go to the emergency room?"

He nodded. She quickly gathered her purse and pulled the keys from the ignition before he changed his mind, but he grabbed her wrist to stop her from getting out of the car.

"There's a catch."

As though verbally walking on eggs, she asked, "What kind of catch?"

"I'll go into the emergency room and take the tests to prove to you I don't have an ulcer if you come back to Kimball and Knight and work out your two weeks' notice."

"That's blackmail."

"That's the deal."

She scowled at him. And saw the sheen of sweat on his forehead, the dull look of pain in his eyes. What was two weeks, she reasoned, compared with Turner's health? Tugging the strap of her purse over her shoulder, she shoved his car keys inside the purse and snapped it shut.

"All right," she said. "You have a deal. I'll work the two weeks if you have a doctor examine you tonight."

He held out his right hand to clinch the bargain, wincing when the movement hurt. "I usually don't deal in oral contracts, but in this case, I think this one will be binding."

Emma hesitated, something in his voice making her wonder what exactly she was agreeing to, then she held out her own right hand. His fingers closed around her smaller hand with a gentle pressure, his eyes gleaming as though he'd just made the deal of a lifetime.

When he finally released her hand and opened his car door, Emma didn't immediately move to get out of the car. She should be feeling triumph or at least a bit of satisfaction that she'd gotten him to agree to be seen by a doctor. For some reason, she was experiencing an odd apprehension, as though she wasn't entirely sure what she'd just agreed to do. She almost wished they had taken the time to make out a written contract so she could have read the fine print before signing it.

Turner had walked around the front of the car while she'd been debating with herself and opened her door. "If I'm going to be poked and prodded for the next hour or so," he said, "you're going to wait on those uncomfortable chairs they make just for hospital waiting rooms, not out here enjoying the soft leather seat of my car."

Tightening her grip on the shoulder strap of her purse, she slid out of the car and locked it. She jerked her head up to stare at him when he took her hand as they started to walk toward the emergency-room entrance.

"Moral support," he murmured. He didn't say another word to her throughout the check-in process, until he was summoned by a nurse who towered over him by at least four inches and outweighed him by perhaps fifty pounds.

Placing his hands on the arms of Emma's chair, he leaned down and said close to her ear, "If I'm not back by midnight, send out the National Guard."

She smiled. "You got it."

When the clock on the wall read eleven-thirty, Emma was beginning to wonder if she was going to have to make good on her promise to Turner. After the first hour of waiting, she'd read every magazine available, even the ones that were two years old and contained every little tidbit of information anyone would ever want to know about golf. The second hour, she began to pace, getting an occasional scowl from an elderly man every time she passed his chair. By eleven, she was starting to really worry and had worked herself into a fine state bordering on panic.

Her imagination ran riot. Maybe it wasn't an ulcer but something even more serious. They could be operating on him at that very moment, and no one would tell her because she wasn't any relation to Turner. That made her think of his family. If Turner was seriously ill, his brothers, his sister, and his father should all be notified. She bit her lip when she realized she didn't know how to get in touch with them. She stopped pacing. Linda would know. His secretary would have all the personal data concerning Turner's relatives. But how would she get in touch with Linda at this hour of the night?

"The phone book," she muttered. She had no idea what Linda's husband's name was and hoped there weren't too many Stricklands listed.

She was debating whether to call right away when the elderly man spoke, his voice as rough as sandpaper. "Lady, would you mind?"

"Excuse me?"

"I would be more than happy if you would kindly stop marching up and down in front of me. I had a headache when I came in here and you ain't helping it any. Either park it or take it outside."

"Sorry," she mumbled, and started back toward the chair she was beginning to hate.

"Emma?"

She spun around. Turner was standing in the doorway of the waiting room. Relief, impatience, frustration, and desire were all part of the emotions churning inside her as she jumped over the grouchy man's outstretched legs and hurried toward Turner.

She had to touch him, to make sure it was really him standing in front of her and not some figment of her imagination. She stopped only a few inches from him, looked into his eyes for a second, then wrapped her arms around his neck to hug him.

"I've been going crazy waiting," she said against his throat, relieved to feel his pulse beating strongly against her lips. "Are you all right?"

The shock of having Emma pressed against him only lasted as long as it took for him to put his arms around her to keep her there.

"The miracles of modern medicine have come through," he said. "They've given me some great stuff that took away the pain. Considering what I've been through the last couple of hours, I should have held out for four weeks as your part of the bargain."

Moving her hands to his shoulders, she pulled back so she could meet his gaze. "I was imagining all sorts of things. I was even about to call Linda to get in touch with your family. What took so long?"

"We complain that the wheels of justice are slow. The medical profession could use a few pointers from the judicial system. There was a lot of waiting in between tests and a nurse trying to get my clothes off and technicians and a couple of doctors hooking me up to various gadgets and taking X-rays."

Considering what he'd been through the last few hours, she barely resisted the urge to shake him. "I know how long you've been in there. What was the verdict?"

He grinned. "I think it's called a diagnosis."

"All right. What was the diagnosis?" she said impatiently. "Are you okay? What did they say was wrong with you? You're not going to have to stay in the hospital, are you?"

"I never knew you could talk so fast, Emma. Or had such an active imagination." Since he detected temper in her eyes along with genuine concern, he told her what she wanted to know. "You were right, but I would appreciate it if you didn't say I told you so. Your research was right on the money. I have an ulcer."

"You make it sound as though that's what I wanted you to have," she said crossly. "What does the doctor recommend you do for it?"

He held up a small paper sack and jiggled it. She could hear the sound of rattling pills and plastic containers hitting each other.

She still wasn't satisfied. "Some of the recommendations in the books I read mentioned bland diets and eliminating stress."

Turner was again amazed that he was enjoying her fussing over him. But he'd had enough of the antiseptic smells that seemed to be clinging to his skin. Keeping one arm around her, he guided her toward the exit. "Let's get out of here before that nurse decides she wants another look at my chest."

As they walked Emma noticed little signs that

proved Turner was feeling better. He was standing upright, his stride normal. Maybe a little too normal, for she had to hurry to keep up with him. His breathing was slow and steady, his color healthy.

When they reached his car, he walked around to the passenger side and waited for her to unlock the doors.

She stared at him over the top of the car. "You don't want to drive?"

He shook his head. "The stuff they gave me was pretty strong. I'm not supposed to operate any mechanical devices."

Emma started the car and backed out of the parking slot. Turner didn't say anything until she was about to turn right on East Santa Clara. "Turn left."

"But you live in the other direction."

"True, but in order to get to your house, we need to go left."

"My house? Why do you want to go back to my house?"

His smile was slow, his eyes glittering in the reflected light from other vehicles. "I'm spending the night on your couch, unless you invite me into your bed. You're going to set your alarm and wake me in four hours so I can take some more of this medicine. Aside from the fact that I'm liable to have another attack if I have to look at those ugly green walls in my apartment in my delicate condition, I need tender, loving care, and you're going to provide it."

"That wasn't part of the deal," she protested.

He put his hand to his side. "I'm not supposed to have any stress, remember?"

Emma had to bite her lip to keep from letting off a little of her own pent-up stress and flicked on the left turn signal. She didn't say a thing.

Turner smiled and leaned his head back.

Six

Supposedly the whole idea of Turner spending the night at her place was to ease his stress level. It might have that effect on him, but Emma was about ready for an ulcer by morning.

If she hadn't felt responsible for his diagnosis of an ulcer by having forced him to go to the emergency room, she might have taken him to his own place regardless of what he wanted. But he needed her, and that was enough.

No one had ever needed her before, and she discovered she liked the feeling. Sadie loved her, had taken care of her, but Emma had never felt the older woman needed her.

Emma knew even before they entered her living room that the couch wasn't going to be adequate for Turner. She hadn't purchased it with the thought that there might be an occasion when her tall employer would be sleeping on it. When she told him he should sleep in her bed, she didn't receive any argument, not even a small one just for the sake of politeness. Nor did he use the opportunity to try to persuade her to join him. As she took him upstairs she tried to tell herself she wasn't really feeling disappointed that he didn't want her to sleep with him.

He removed his jeans and shirt as she turned down the covers, then he slid between the cool sheets, wearing only white briefs. Emma thought she took the whole procedure of his preparing for bed rather well. At least on the outside. Inside, she was a bowl of mush.

Almost as soon as his dark head hit the pillow, his eyes closed and his breathing became slow and deep.

She stood beside the bed for a few minutes looking down at him as he slept. Once she got past the astonishment of seeing Turner Knight in her bed, she was able to recognize the extent of his exhaustion from fighting the pain of his ulcer for so long. What she didn't understand was why he'd fought it instead of doing something about it.

For herself, she leaned down and smoothed the sheet and quilt over him. Even in sleep, his strong personality drew her like a magnet, his physical beauty nearly taking her breath away. The temptation to lie down beside him was almost overwhelming, and before she gave in to it, she turned away.

The linen closet was on the other side of her studio, and as she passed the open doorway she remembered the look on Turner's face when he'd stared down at the drawing on the board. Perhaps if she didn't have the same longings to express her innermost feelings by creating something from within herself, she wouldn't have recognized his expression. Her suspicions had been proved when he'd redrawn the boy. His innate talent was incredible.

Wondering why Turner had looked so tortured in her studio kept her from deep, restful sleep during the four hours before he was due to have more of his medication. Dragon accompanied her up the stairs after she shook out the dosage of medication. She touched his shoulder and called his name softly without any effect at all. She fought the temptation to stroke her fingers over the warm flesh under her hand, and shook him a little harder than necessary because of her desire.

He opened his eyes and focused on her face, then on the white nightshirt she wore. After a moment he looked at her face. "You didn't have any clothes on a minute ago."

The rough huskiness of his voice sent flashes of heat shimmering down her spine. The implication that he'd been dreaming about her was responsible for her hand shaking as she handed him the tablets and glass of water. She was thankful he was too drowsy to notice as he swallowed the medication, rolled onto his side with his back toward her, and returned to his dream.

Dragon jumped up on the opposite side of the bed and padded over to the male figure occupying the space Emma usually used. The dog didn't seem to mind the change in occupant as she settled down on the covers in front of Turner's chest, leaning into the man's warmth.

Emma was turning away to leave the room when she heard Turner murmur her name. His arm wrapped around Dragon and snuggled the little dog closer. She didn't know whether to laugh or sigh when she realized Turner was mistaking an eighteen-pound bundle of fur for her.

Returning to the couch, she reset the alarm for six o'clock and tried to get comfortable on the short couch. Lack of sleep eventually allowed her to shut down her thoughts of how she would handle her overnight houseguest in the morning, and she escaped into a deep sleep.

The aroma of coffee roused her several hours later, but it took the breath being knocked out of her from Dragon's pounce onto her stomach to waken her fully. Pushing her dog away with a grumbled reprimand, Emma groggily got to her feet. Because it required all of the few faculties working just to make her way to the kitchen, she didn't give a thought to her appearance.

It was the first thing Turner noticed when he turned from the refrigerator he'd been peering into and saw her leaning against the door frame. Her gorgeous hair was tousled and tangled from a restless night, exactly how he imagined it would look after he spent hours making love to her. Several buttons down the front of her nightshirt were undone and the shirttail hem draped down to just above her knees. Her small feet were bare. As bare as she must be underneath the cotton fabric.

Bringing his gaze up to her face, he tested the water. "Good morning."

"Hmmm," she murmured.

"Are you usually this outgoing in the morning?"

She took a deep breath as she pushed herself away from the support of the door frame. "Actually, I'm fairly cheerful as a rule. But then I usually get more than a few hours of sleep."

With unerring accuracy, Turner opened the cupboard to his right and took down a mug with a yellow smiley face painted on it. He poured coffee into it from the pot on the counter.

"Maybe this will help," he said, smiling as he walked toward her.

She took the mug from him, wrapping both hands around it to keep from reaching out to stroke the bare chest in front of her. She nearly burned her tongue when she took a sip too soon. Damn, she thought, feeling like a fool. Why did he have to stand so close, smell so male, and have no more clothes on than a pair of jeans?

He leaned down and touched her mouth with his. He repeated his earlier greeting, this time in a low intimate murmur. "Good morning."

Emma couldn't have answered if her life or his depended on it. He was too close, too compellingly attractive, too much too early in the morning when her defenses were almost nonexistent. She could only meet his direct gaze and feel the heat emanating from his body so close to hers.

Even though he knew her silence wasn't an invitation, Turner bent his head again and took the taste of her he'd been wanting so badly for far too long. He was demanding, yet tender as he thrust his fingers into her hair, tilting her head enough for him to take the kiss deeper.

Emma thought she heard thunder even though it was a clear day. Then she realized it was her heart thudding loudly in her chest as she managed to set the mug down. Her hands felt as though they were burning from the heat of his skin as she ran them up over his chest to wrap her arms around his neck.

The action crushed her breasts against him,

and Turner nearly lost the fragile control he'd needed since she first appeared at the door. Her scent reminded him of sleepy Sunday mornings at Knight's Keep, lavender and sunlight emanating from the linens on the bed. She tasted like hot nights and warm whiskey, and he was dazed by the intoxicating hunger of her natural response.

He'd felt desire before, but never this craving, this desperate need to claim a woman as his by the most intimate way possible between a man and a woman. He'd ached before. He'd needed a woman before. But he'd never experienced all of those things at the same time, never with the intensity he was feeling for this fragile woman he finally held in his arms.

"Turner," she gasped, not asking a question or wanting an answer. His name was enough.

He buried his face in her hair, the yearning in her voice vibrating through him. Knowing he could take her, that she was as willing as he was to satisfy the mutual desire, he almost lost his grasp on the thin thread of control. It was too soon to let her go, to look into her eyes and see the need he knew was there. He'd tasted it.

He simply held her trembling body tightly against his until his heartbeat and his breathing leveled.

Slowly he lifted his head and looked down at her. "We're going to do something about this. And soon. You know that, don't you?"

She shook her head. "I don't know anything at the moment." Her eyes widened. "Should you be doing this? What about your ulcer?"

He smiled. "I'm not feeling any pain at all, not the kind you mean."

Emma ached with unfulfilled desire herself, and with knowing their attraction couldn't go any further than it already had.

"We can't do this."

He didn't agree. "We already are."

"I mean go any further than this."

"What you mean is you don't think we should give in to the physical attraction between us. I disagree. I can't think of anything more right than you and I making love."

"Turner," she said hesitantly, unsure of how to make him understand. "There are things you don't know about me, things that would make a difference to you if we became involved."

"We've been involved with each other for two years, Emma. It's just lately that we allowed ourselves to admit it." His hold on her tightened. "Tell me, Emma. Aloud. Tell me you want me as much as I want you."

"Yes!" she almost shouted, goaded beyond caution. "I want you so badly I lie awake at night wondering what it would be like. But I've accepted that I can't always have everything I want."

The ringing of the phone jangled their taut nerves and cut through the tension between them. When Turner's arms didn't relax their hold on her, she said, "I have to answer that."

"Who would be calling you this early in the morning?"

"My neighbor. She's expecting a baby any day now, and her husband is out of town."

He released her, satisfied another man wouldn't

be on the other end of the phone line. "We aren't through with this discussion, Emma."

She met his gaze. "I know."

He watched her as she moved her mug to the counter and was pleased to see her hand wasn't steady. He was feeling a little rocky, too, and it had nothing to do with his newly diagnosed ulcer. He wandered over to the refrigerator and resumed his examination of its contents while he unabashedly listened to Emma's end of the conversation.

Picking up the receiver, Emma asked, "Are you all right, Audrey?"

"I was just going to ask you the same thing. Other than carrying around what seems like a large bowling ball, I'm in fine shape. No water breaking or labor pains. That's not why I'm phoning."

Emma slumped against the wall and took a deep breath of relief. "Give me a minute. When I heard the phone, visions of every Lamaze class I took with you flashed before my eyes, then my mind went blank."

"Since you did pick up the phone, you've already answered the question I had, which was are you all right? There's a flashy black Porsche parked in your driveway, the same one that was there when I went to bed at eight o'clock last night. It's only six-thirty, and well, dammit, Emma, you've never had anyone spend the night before. I've never known you to have any company at all except me. I wanted to make sure you were okay, and now that I know, I'll stop worrying and can go back to persuading this child to be born."

Before Emma could explain who the Porsche belonged to and why it was still in her driveway at the break of dawn, Audrey had hung up.

Replacing the receiver, she made a sound of impatience and irritation.

Turner lifted his head from the view of the refrigerator's insides. "Problem?"

She shook her head. "Not really. At least not with her pregnancy. She was just checking to make sure the person who owns the black car in my driveway is supposed to be here."

"Does she usually check out all your visitors?"

"There haven't been all that many, which is why she was concerned when she saw your car."

A curious light entered his eyes, changing them from cobalt to a deep cerulean. "How many have there been?"

"I already told you," she said crossly. "Not many. Are you going to stand in front of that open refrigerator door all day? Either take something out or shut the door."

He grinned. "I'm going to take a wild guess and say not many visitors as in one. Me. I'm right, aren't I? My car is the only one that's ever been in your driveway the next morning."

Picking up her coffee mug from the counter, she took a long swallow, then grimaced because the coffee was now cold. She dumped the contents into the sink and poured fresh coffee into the mug. She carried it with her as she walked across the tile floor toward the doorway. "Save your browbeating for the courtroom, counselor. I'm going to take a shower. If you find anything you want for breakfast, help yourself."

He shut the refrigerator door, the sound drawing

her gaze back to him as she stopped in the doorway. "I'm going to pass on breakfast," he said. It only took two strides for him to be in front of her. Looking down at her, he complained lightly, "There's no meat or pastry, Emma. Couldn't you buy even one measly little donut?"

"There was a time when about all I had to eat were donuts," she said without thinking, "and I vowed never to have another donut once I had a choice." When she realized what she'd said, she tried to cover it over by adding, "Donuts have a lot of fat and calories in them."

As he looked down into her eyes he could see a glimpse of the original Emma, the one who was so adept at shutting people out. He never wanted to see her do that to him again, and that's why he backed off. This time. But soon he was going to have answers to all the questions that had cropped up during the last couple of days.

"I'll take a rain check on breakfast," he said. "I'm going back to my apartment to shower and get dressed for work."

"Should you be working today?"

"The doctor told me I could work as long as I took the medicine and lightened up on the stress." He touched her because it was a necessary response. She tensed because it was an automatic response. "Since you aren't ready for me to join you in your shower, I'll have to go home to take one all alone."

Emma hated to sound as though she was fussing again, but she had to know. "What about driving? You had your medication only two hours ago."

"The stuff they prescribed isn't as strong as the medication they gave me at the hospital. It's safe for me to drive on my own."

"Then you're not in pain?"

"A little," he admitted, amazed how much it warmed him that Emma was concerned about him. "The medication will take a few days to fully kick in."

She didn't look convinced but didn't argue. "Then I'll see you at the office."

She started to turn away. The coffee sloshed in her cup when he stopped her with a hand on her forearm.

He met the question in her eyes with a serious expression in his own. "I know I gave you a hard time last night about going to the emergency room. I don't believe I thanked you for forcing me to get the attention I needed." His lips curved upward a little. "And I haven't thanked you for the use of your bed either." He ran the back of a finger over her satin-smooth cheek. "Although it would have been even better if you had been there with me."

"You're welcome," she replied, ignoring the last part of his statement.

Turner looked down at her. At the office she would be the other Emma. He wanted the Emma who responded to him like kerosene to a match. He wanted more than a kiss from her, but that would have to do for now.

Threading his fingers through her hair, he clenched his hand into a loose fist and gently pulled her head back to give him access to her mouth. He took full advantage of the protest she was about to make by hungrily kissing her parted lips.

All too soon he raised his head, gave her one last long glance, then walked out of the kitchen.

Emma leaned back against the wall, her body stiff with tension and unfulfilled desire. When she heard the front door close, she took a deep steadying breath, but she didn't move away from the support of the wall until she heard the powerful Porsche drive away.

Walking into her living room, she stared at the books lining her walls. Those books had helped her through many situations in the past, answered a number of important questions for her, but she wasn't going to find any solutions between the covers of a book this time. The emotion she'd labeled infatuation was a dim term for the feelings Turner created within her when his mouth covered hers.

Or when he touched her. Or when he looked at her. Or when he was in the same room. Or when she thought about him.

She loved him.

She might not be overly familiar with that particular emotion, but it was the only word that explained the wrenching worry she'd experienced last night at the hospital, the secure feeling in the early hours of the morning when she thought of the man who was sleeping under her roof. He was impatient with imperfection, occasionally arrogant when he wanted something done immediately, and put too much emphasis on his work.

And she was in love with him.

She couldn't imagine anything more crazy than loving a man who came from a radically different background from hers. The differences between them were so extreme, they might as well have come from two planets. It shouldn't matter, but deep inside her remained remnants of the young insecure girl who had lived on the streets. She'd come a long way from the child in ragged clothing who'd raided Dumpsters behind a bakery for something to eat. But there was enough of that little girl left in her mind for her to realize it was foolish of her even to consider any type of permanent relationship with Turner.

Her mouth twisted in a grimace of self-mockery. Not that he'd so much as hinted that he was interested in anything other than a one-night stand.

Most of her life, she'd settled for what she could have, until Sadie had convinced her she could have whatever she wanted if she worked hard enough to get it. Sadie had taught her to go after what she wanted. It wasn't going to be handed to her. Emma had discovered that Sadie had been right, but this time her happiness depended on someone else. And Turner would only be interested in a temporary arrangement.

If he knew of her background, he might not even want that.

Although she had never resorted to prostitution as some of the other homeless girls had, the way she'd had to live would be unacceptable to many people. Sadie had told Emma never to be ashamed of having less than others. The older woman had also told her there would be people who wouldn't feel the same way.

Thinking of Sadie made Emma realize she hadn't seen her for almost a week. The last time was several nights before she'd handed in her resignation. Sadie had coughed many times, a deep rasping cough that alarmed Emma. They had argued when Sadie refused to come home with her or even let her take her to a doctor.

A low growl interrupted her thoughts, and Emma looked down at her little dog, who was sitting only inches away from her feet. "All right, Dragon. I'll feed you. Then I have to get ready for work."

After she'd fed the dog, she walked into her bedroom, her gaze going to the rumpled bed, her thoughts on the man who'd spent half the night there. Feeling the need to tidy her surroundings when her mind was in such a turmoil, she wrenched the sheets off the bed and stuffed them in the hamper before remaking the bed with fresh linens.

Hating the edgy tension that was remaining with her even though Turner had left, she went into the bathroom and turned on the shower. But even here she couldn't escape from Turner. It was too easy for her to imagine him standing under the water, streams sluicing over his bare skin the same as they were over hers. Easy to imagine him taking a bar of soap and rubbing it over the muscular chest she'd felt against her sensitive breasts, grazing his strong thighs, soaping every inch of his body.

Even though the water was merely warm, she felt smothered as though she were in a steam bath. Her skin was flushed, her blood simmering in her veins.

She turned off the hot water and gasped when streams of cold water hit her overheated body. She raised her face into the spray, hoping the shock would jolt some sense into her. It didn't work.

What she needed was a dose of cold reality. After work, she would go looking for Sadie.

Later that evening Turner stalked across the grass separating Emma's house from her neighbor's. The woman who had phoned that morning either lived in this house or one of the others in the cul-de-sac. He hadn't thought to ask, but then he hadn't realized it would be necessary to know where Emma's pregnant friend lived.

The only reason he could think of for Emma's absence was that she had taken her neighbor to the hospital. She hadn't mentioned any plans for the evening at the office, but then she never had before. And he hadn't asked. It had been business as usual, as though the night before had never taken place. He'd been as guilty of behaving that way as she had. There was a ton of work to get through, and for the first time in weeks, he wasn't waylaid by pain in his stomach.

Around ten that morning Emma had reminded him to take his medicine. He'd frowned at her and told her he wasn't a child.

He'd seen the momentary hurt in her eyes, then she'd shut down. The few occasions he'd seen her during the rest of the day, she'd been the efficient, distant paralegal he'd hoped had been banished by their new relationship. Knowing he was responsible for her converting back to the original version of Emma didn't make him hate it any less.

He rang the doorbell of the neat two-story house next to Emma's and waited with his hands shoved into the pockets of the tan jacket he'd thrown on just before leaving his apartment. When no one came to the door, he rang again. If there hadn't been any lights on inside, he would have left and tried the neighbor on the other side. The sound of music and laughter could be heard, too, although faintly. A television set was on.

If this was Emma's friend, she wasn't very sociable. Or else the lights and television had been left on in the rush to get the expectant mother to the hospital. He cursed under his breath. He hated not knowing where Emma was or what she was doing.

The door was finally opened but only a few inches, a safety chain strung across the opening. A woman with coal-black hair skimmed away from her face and braided into a thick long rope that draped over her shoulder looked up at him with curious dark eyes. A turquoise amulet dangled from a chain over her white cotton top and chunks of the same stone danced on slim silver threads fashioned into earrings.

"I'm looking for a friend of Emma Valerian's named Audrey."

Frowning, she said, "I'm Audrey Twosteps. Why?"

"I'm looking for Emma. She isn't home. Have you seen her this evening?"

The woman suddenly smiled, her eyes widening with humor and surprise. "Ah, the black Porsche. Just a second." The door was shut, the chain unlatched, then she pulled the door open again. "Come in. I would like nothing better than for the neighbors to see a handsome stranger on my doorstep, especially that snoopy Miss Grayville on the corner, but standing isn't my favorite thing these days."

Turner had seen women in various stages of pregnancy, wives of acquaintances, business associates, female lawyers, and other lawyers' wives, but he was slightly alarmed by the sight of this woman's very pregnant frame.

As though she were fragile crystal, he took her arm and led her away from the door. "Are you all right?"

She chuckled. "Good Lord, you're as bad as my husband. I'm having a baby." His grip tightened on her arm. She stopped and glanced up at him, seeing the stricken look in his eyes. "Not now, for heaven's sake. Relax."

He took several deep breaths as she settled awkwardly into an upholstered armchair in her living room. As though it were his house instead of hers, he asked, "Would you like a glass of water or something?"

She gestured with her hand for him to sit on the couch, amusement glinting in her eyes. "Nothing for me, thanks. I'd offer you something, but you don't look the type who would care for guava juice and that's all I've got on hand. My husband, Dory, says he wishes I'd crave something decent like chocolate milk, which he loves."

"Nothing for me, thanks."

"You wanted to know if I've seen Emma."

He sat on the edge of the couch and rested his forearms on his thighs. "Since she obviously isn't taking you to the hospital, I was hoping you knew where she was or when she might be home."

"She reported in about twenty minutes ago. I had

a doctor's appointment early this morning and the doctor said the baby was in position, so I won't be waiting much longer. I told Emma what the doctor said when she phoned at noon to check up on me, and she's been calling every hour since then. I guess she doesn't want to waste those Lamaze classes we took."

"It's none of my business, so you don't have to answer if you don't want to, but why is Emma going to be your Lamaze coach and not your husband?"

"Dory drives for a trucking firm. He's been trying to arrange to take only short hauls during the last couple of weeks, but just in case he's out of town and can't get back in time, Emma took on the job as my coach. Dory went through the classes with his previous wife when she had his first son. He said it's like riding a bike. It'll come back to him when the time comes. Between him calling every time he stops for gas and Emma calling every hour, I can hardly get out the front door to get the mail."

"You were saying Emma called you twenty minutes ago. Do you know where she was calling from?"

For the first time since she'd answered the door, Emma's neighbor didn't immediately answer him. Her dark exotic eyes studied him thoroughly before she asked, "Has Emma told you about Sadie?"

He shook his head. "Who's Sadie?"

Audrey didn't answer him directly. "I knew Emma for over a year before she told me about Sadie. You should hear about her from Emma, not me."

"I've known her for two years," he stated, looking down at his clasped hands for a moment. Straightening, he placed his hands on his thighs and got to his feet. "I'm beginning to realize I don't know her at all."

"That can change only if you want it to change."

"She has to want it, too, or it won't work."

Tilting her head to one side, Audrey asked, "Are you Turner Knight? The lawyer she works for?"

"Yes. I'm sorry. I should have introduced myself earlier."

Grinning, Audrey shook her head. "It was more fun to invite a tall, dark, handsome stranger into my house. We old married pregnant ladies have to get our kicks where we can." She suddenly turned serious. "You have your work cut out for you with Emma if she means more to you than a good employee. Considering you spent the night with her, I'm jumping to the conclusion that she does. She's the most private person I've ever met. She doesn't trust people very much, but once she does, she's the most loyal, giving, generous person I've known. Underneath that practical exterior is a very sensitive soul. I wouldn't like to think you're the type of man to take advantage of that."

Turner leaned down and lifted one of Audrey's hands from the arm of the chair and held it between his. "I don't know what's going to happen between me and Emma, but I can promise you I will do everything in my power not to hurt her."

Her fingers tightened briefly around his, then she withdrew her hand. "It isn't me you have to convince. Please sit down. You're giving me a kink in my neck and I have enough kinks going for me. I certainly don't need another one."

He smiled but shook his head. "As much as I'd like to give your Miss Grayville something to think about, I need to try to find Emma."

"If you'll sit down for five minutes, I'll give you a few ideas of where to start."

Turner sat.

Seven

Turner hadn't given much thought to the areas of San Jose Audrey had sent him to other than how vague her instructions had been. He was to go to these places and drive within a six-block radius while checking both sides of the streets and any parking lots for Emma's car. He would drive all night if necessary to see Emma and apologize for snapping at her at work. After the first hour behind the wheel, he thought it might come to that.

Following Audrey's directions, he saw parts of the city he'd never been to before and a life-style he hadn't realized existed in such great numbers. Turner had read about the growing number of homeless people in the newspapers and caught glimpses of the occasional news special on television concerned with the growing problem all over the country.

Now it was in front of him, behind him, offering to wash his windshield for a dollar.

Driving through the sections Audrey had directed him to opened his eyes to the conditions in which homeless individuals wandering the streets of San Jose lived. The sight of a tiny elderly woman pushing a heavily laden shopping cart that seemed too much of a burden for her slight frame made him want to stop the car and help her. He saw a man huddled against the cement frame of a freeway underpass, his arms wrapped around a bundle that could very well be everything he owned. A woman with three small children climbed into a car up on blocks in a vacant lot. The car wasn't going anywhere and neither were they.

Guilt didn't sit very well with Turner, but he didn't know what else to call it. He'd been so busy being self-involved in his own little legal world, he hadn't taken the time to see what was happening in the city where he lived.

It made him wonder what else he'd neglected to see while trying to make a name for himself in corporate law.

And he was completely mystified as to why Audrey would think Emma would be in any of the places she'd sent him to that night.

After looking in the first two locations, he turned around to drive to the last section of town Audrey had suggested. He didn't have much hope left of finding Emma, but he would rather be looking for her than be back in his apartment, pacing the malignant green carpet or staring at the ugly walls.

And wanting her.

He passed a shopping center as directed and looked for Emma's car on both sides of San Carlos. He was about to give it up as a lost cause when he finally spotted her small car as he glanced at vehicles parked next to a small diner. It was either hers or one very much like it.

At the next intersection he made a U-turn so he would be on the same side of the street as the parked car he hoped was Emma's. It had to be hers. He was running out of places to look.

Audrey hadn't thought it was strange that he was anxious to find Emma. At least she'd been tactful enough not to ask for any reasons. He knew he wasn't going to get that same acceptance from Emma. She would want to know why he'd come looking for her.

He doubted if she was ready to hear his answer.

Turning into the parking lot next to the diner, he found an empty slot near the front. A couple of letters flickered in the red neon sign above the door that announced the diner was open all night. As he turned off the engine he no longer had to wonder where Emma was. She was sitting in one of the vinyl-covered booths the color of yellow ochre near the front window. And she wasn't alone. An older woman was seated across from her.

Something loosened inside him when he saw Emma. Her hair was tied back with a rolled red handkerchief, and she was wearing her glasses. He could see the collar of her white shirt was pulled up around her neck, her shoulders covered with a tan tweed jacket that showed definite signs of wear on the cuffs and lapels.

She fit in perfectly with the other customers lounging in the booths.

He turned his attention to the woman she was with. The first thing he noticed was that the woman's gray hair seemed to have been arranged by a tornado. He counted three scarves wrapped around her neck and hanging down the front of a once elegant black coat that had a bedraggled fur collar. Even from this distance, he could see the shiny worn splotches on the shoulders and elbows. The coat fit similarly to the one worn by the elderly lady he had seen pushing the shopping cart earlier. It had taken him a second look to realize the woman had been wearing two coats over several dresses.

Apparently Emma's companion adhered to the same fashion style. And like the woman with the shopping cart, she was a resident of the streets.

The woman suddenly began coughing into a man's large white handkerchief, and Turner saw the way Emma stiffened and clenched her fingers on the edge of the table. Then her shoulders slumped, and she leaned on her elbows, holding her head in her hands as the women kept coughing.

What in the hell was Emma doing there? Turner wondered, and came up with his own answer. The woman sitting across from Emma must be Sadie.

He took the keys out of the ignition and stuffed them into the side pocket of his jacket. The time had come to push. Emma wasn't going to like it, but that was just too damn bad. He wasn't going through another night like this one, wondering and worrying, especially now that he knew she spent time in places like this at all hours of the night.

Emma waited until Sadie caught her breath after her latest coughing spell. She knew the older woman would turn her down again, but she had to try.

"Dammit, Sadie. I wish you would come back to my place so I can take care of you."

"I've told you a thousand times not to swear, child," Sadie scolded in a voice husky from coughing and too many cigarettes. "I'm just fine."

"I can see that."

It took Sadie several attempts of striking a match against the large box of kitchen matches she'd taken from a coat pocket before it flared into a flickering flame. She touched the lighted match to the end of an unfiltered cigarette.

Coughing briefly, she smiled at Emma. "Too many cigarettes, that's all."

"Then why don't you give them up?"

Sadie waved away a cloud of smoke. "I wish you would get yourself a husband and a houseful of children, Emma. Then you'd have someone else to fret over and leave me alone."

Emma straightened and sat back against the booth. "You've been saying that a lot lately, that you want me to leave you alone. I know why you're saying it, Sadie, and it's not going to work. We've been through too much together for me to abandon you when you need me. You've brought me up better than that."

She heard someone enter the diner behind her, crossing the floor to sit on a stool at the counter. Sadie gave the newcomer a long hard look before turning her gaze back to Emma.

"You keep telling me you never see any interesting men," Sadie said. "There's a sharp-looking guy that just came in that's the type of man you should get to know. Clean, healthy, and by the looks of the watch he's wearing, has money. What's wrong with someone like him?"

Emma glanced over her shoulder and gasped

when she recognized the man leaning on one of the counter stools. His long legs were stretched out in front of him with one ankle crossed over the other, his arms folded across his chest. And he was looking directly at her.

"Turner! What are you doing here?"

He smiled fleetingly. "Why shouldn't I be here? This is one of my favorite late-night dining spots."

She stared at him. "It is not. You were following me."

He shook his head. "If I had been following you, I'd have been here sooner." He nodded at the cup of coffee in front of her. "How's the coffee?"

"You should know," she said. "You come here all the time."

He gave her an unabashed grin and turned to tell the plump man behind the counter that he wanted a decaf coffee. After he paid for his order, he carried the cup and saucer over to the booth. "Aren't you going to introduce me to your friend?"

As if she had a choice, Emma thought irritably. "Sadie, this is Turner Knight of Kimball and Knight, the firm I used to work for."

"Still work for," Turner corrected her.

The older woman frowned. "Good Lord, a lawyer. Forget my recommendation. You'll have to throw this one back, Em. I don't want you getting involved with any lawyer."

Pulling a chair away from a nearby table, Turner turned it around with the back facing the booth and sat down. He placed the cup and saucer on the table and crossed his arms over the top of the chair back. "She can't throw me back. I'm already caught."

Sadie leaned toward Emma. "You never told me you were seriously involved with anyone."

"That's because I'm not," Emma said firmly, giving Turner a scalding look.

Again Turner corrected her. "She doesn't think I'm serious, but I am."

The older woman slumped back against the booth, slowly shaking her head, "You're a grown woman. I just hope you know what you're doing."

Emma's hands clenched around the edge of the table. The strain of trying to remain calm was apparent in her voice. "I'm not doing anything with him, Sadie."

"What's wrong with me?" Turner asked.

"You're a lawyer," Sadie said.

"Why would being a lawyer be a problem? Practicing law is what I do, not who I am."

"Very pretty answer," Sadie said. "And quick. You're a lawyer all right."

"What have you got against lawyers?"

"How long have you got?"

Amused, Turner said, "As long as it takes."

For a few seconds Sadie's gray eyes assessed and weighed Turner with such thoroughness, he had to fight the urge to squirm in his chair.

After the older woman had put a match to yet another cigarette and blew the smoke up into the air above them, she directed her sharp gaze on him again and said, "The trouble with most lawyers is they pay too much attention to the law and not to the people they represent. They find the law code that suits their purpose, argue their case, and when they win, they act as if they'd personally scored the victory, not considering that the law is the winner. They look at their clients as a reason to fight, to argue, to charge ridiculously high fees, whether they believe in the client's cause or not. Winning is the thing. In most instances, if they'd continued looking for precedents of similar cases, they could have won the case to the benefit of the other side, not themselves."

He'd heard complaints such as hers before, although not put as well as she had. "You sound like someone who's lost a case."

Sadie didn't take offense. Just the opposite. She laughed, which made her cough into the white handkerchief again.

Turner looked at Emma and saw the rigid way she was holding herself, the deep concern in her eyes as she watched her friend gasp for breath.

When Sadie finally recovered, she smiled at Turner. "I lost more than one case because I kept thinking of the client instead of the fee I would make. The law firms I worked for didn't agree with my standard of practice. The last set of partners ended up suing me when I took on a class-action suit that received a lot of adverse publicity. The bloodsuckers took everything I had."

To give Turner his due, he didn't show the astonishment he was feeling. "You're a lawyer?"

"Was," the older woman rasped. "A darn good one, too, if I do say so myself." She shrugged her shoulders, although the action didn't move the layers of clothing all that much. "Now I give free legal advice to people who really need it and who can't afford a high-priced attorney who pays forty bucks for a haircut and wears expensive watches."

"Not all lawyers are parasites who feed off the

misfortune of others," he argued. "A few of us like to think we perform a necessary function in society."

Sadie nodded. "I see. Is that why you don't draw or paint? You think you contribute more to society's laws than you would to its culture?"

"I'm not an artist. I'm a despicable lawyer, remember?"

"You can't be both? I know the law, sonny. There isn't a statute on any books that states an individual doesn't have the right to practice two occupations at the same time on the condition both are legal pursuits. The last time I checked, being a lawyer and an artist were respectable professions."

Turner glanced at Emma, then back at Sadie. "You must have misunderstood Emma. My father is the artist, not me."

Shaking her head, Sadie didn't accept that explanation. "Em told me what you did with her sketch of the little boy and about the expression on your face while you were drawing. She also mentioned the visit to the hospital and the diagnosis of an ulcer. If a man is happy in his chosen profession, then why would he be eating himself alive from the inside with an ulcer? Something you love isn't supposed to hurt you. It should fulfill you and make you happy."

Turner stared at Emma's friend for a long moment. Finally he murmured, "I'm glad I never had to argue a case against you in court. You go for the jugular."

"Sometimes wounds have to bleed before they can heal." Sadie shoved the pack of cigarettes into a pocket of her coat and tied one of the scarves around her head. Looking at Emma, she said, "You've always gone after what you wanted, child. Don't let this time be any different."

Emma gave the older woman a faint smile. "I've been after you to come live with me for two years now and haven't succeeded."

"You don't need me holding you back," she said firmly. "You've gone past the way I want to go and have to go the rest of the way on your own. I told you that when you bought that house. It's right for you, not me."

When Sadie slid out of the booth, Turner stood up and replaced the chair where he'd found it. Offering her his right hand, he said, "It's been a revelation meeting you, Sadie. I hope I see you again."

She extended her hand and clasped his. "Who knows? It's a strange world." Dropping her hand, she turned to Emma, who was also standing. "I would ask you not to worry about me, but I know you will anyway. You've always had too much heart, child. That's why you keep getting it bruised. It's too big a target." She touched the side of Emma's face. "I'll be fine. You of all people know I can handle anything life throws at me."

Emma nodded and put her arms around Sadie for a brief hug. "I left a case of those special blankets behind the diner. I told you about them the last time I saw you."

"Ah, the space-age blanket. Keeps a person warm, is water-resistant, and folds up to fit in your pocket. I'll pass them around. Now stop looking so sad, child. You know I can take care of myself. Put on a smile and sit down with this good-looking man who looks like he could keep you warmer than those spacey blankets."

For a woman who was fifteen pounds under-weight and was wearing two coats and three dres-ses, Sadie could move fast. Turner hardly blinked and the older woman was gone from the diner.

Emma sank back down onto the cushioned seat, her gaze on the woman passing the window. She slowly raised her hand in response to Sadie's wave, then let it fall down onto the tabletop.

Turner would rather have sat next to her, but his instincts told him Emma needed some room, physically and emotionally. He slid onto the cush-ion Sadie had occupied.

Watching her, he silently drank his coffee. The lawyer who paid Emma's paycheck had a stack of questions to ask. The man who wanted to be her lover would wait until she was ready to give him the answers.

The plump man who had poured Turner's coffee came from behind the counter carrying a coffeepot. His shuffling gait as he went from table to table drew Turner's gaze to his feet. The man was wear-ing felt bedroom slippers.

When he reached their booth, he asked, "How about another cup, Em?"

"Thanks, Gus."

He saw Turner reach into his pocket and held up his hand. "No need to pay. Em's family. And you're with her."

After the man had returned to his duties behind the counter, Turner's raised brow asked the ques-tion for him.

Emma toyed with the spoon next to the steaming

cup of coffee. "We're not related. Gus is referring to a different kind of family than you have with your brothers, sister, and father."

He detected a note of defensiveness and sought to eliminate it. "Whatever kind of relationship you have with Gus, Audrey, and Sadie, it seems to be a close one."

"Audrey!" She started fishing around in the pocket of her jeans for some change. "I need to call her."

"You don't need to call her. When I left her about an hour ago, she was fine. She was going to bed and told me to tell you she didn't think anything was going to happen tonight."

"What were you doing at Audrey's?"

"Trying to find you." He knew Emma wasn't going to like this part. "You weren't home, so I tried next door."

"And she told you I would be here?"

"Or a few other places. This one was my last stop." When he saw the hurt and betrayal in her eyes, he added, "That's all Audrey told me. She asked if I knew about Sadie, and when I said no, she said it was up to you to tell me."

"That's like giving a dog a sniff of a bone and then burying it. It only made you more curious when she wouldn't tell you anything about Sadie, didn't it?"

He reached across the table and wrapped his warm fingers around her cold hands. "You don't have to tell me anything if you aren't ready. I can wait."

"It's better to tell you about my background now. Then you'll understand why I said we can't get involved."

"All right, but before you do, I want you to know it doesn't matter. I've gone past the point of no return with you, Emma. Nothing you say is going to make a difference. I want you, and I'm going to have you."

"You want Emma Valerian, but there is no such person. She's pure fiction."

His thumb stroked her wrist, and he smiled when he felt her pulse rate quicken. "She feels very real to me."

His persistence was making it more difficult, Emma thought. Leading him by the hand wasn't working, so she was going to have to hit him over the head to get his attention. "You come from a long line of ancestors dating back to the beginning of time, Turner. I don't even have a last name. Valerian was the brand name on a piece of luggage Sadie found. She thought the name had some class to it, so she tacked it onto my first name when she enrolled me in school."

"Sadie is your mother?"

Emma met his gaze, searching for condemnation or distaste. All she saw was curiosity. She shook her head. "She's sort of a surrogate mother to me and a number of other children who ended up on the streets for one reason or the other. When I was eleven, the leader of the commune I lived in decided there was an uneven number of eleven-year-olds, which was bad for the balance of the group. I don't know how they came to the decision that the odd child was me, but the result was I was dropped off in front of a grade school on the east side of San Jose."

"They just left you there?"

She smiled faintly at the anger she heard in his voice. "From what Sadie has implied, it happens more than it should. Not necessarily in front of a school, but in motels, abandoned cars, at gas stations."

"What did you do?"

"I walked up to the door of the school and went in. A few minutes later I was escorted out. They didn't believe me when I said my name was Embrace, didn't have a last name, no parents, and no home address. I also didn't have any shoes, money, or proper clothes. According to the hatchet-faced woman in the principal's office, wearing a man's T-shirt and nothing else was not the way to dress for school. My hair hadn't been combed for several months and I don't imagine I smelled all that good at the time either."

Turner didn't know what surprised him more, what she was telling him or that she was confiding in him. His smile shared the humor instead of mocking her. "Embrace is better than Lamorek."

A glint of mischief replaced the shadows in her eyes. "Lamorek is your first name?"

He nodded. His eyes narrowed in a threatening stare, which didn't mean much since he was also smiling. "If I ever hear you use it, I'll whip out Embrace in front of Harry and the staff."

She countered his threat with one of her own. "If you do that, I'll sic Sadie on you."

He grinned, held up his hand, and surrendered. "You win. Embrace is forgotten. How did you end up with Sadie?"

Emma tried to keep a straight face but failed. "I fought her over a bagel behind a bakery."

"Did you win?"

"She ended up sharing it with me along with a blanket and a place to sleep. She thought Embrace was pretentious, so she shortened it to Emma. She also made me take a bath in a horse trough located in an apricot grove. She cut off my hair, scrubbed me within an inch of my life, and said it was time to start over since things hadn't worked out too well with my other life."

"I think we need more Sadies and fewer women like the one who escorted you out of the school. So what happened next?"

"I knew how to read and write, but barely. Not enough to get into the sixth grade. Sadie took me and another girl about my age to the library every day and taught us what we needed to know. When she was confident we could handle ourselves with the other kids, she got us all fitted out at a thrift store and enrolled us in school using the address of this diner as our residence. She knew a parolee she'd defended on a forgery charge who provided us with the birth certificates the school required. Somehow she came up with a good story to explain why we didn't have the proper documents or records from other schools."

Having met Sadie, Turner didn't doubt for a minute that she could talk the authorities at a school into believing anything. "Where did you live?"

"Gus has a storeroom out back separate from the diner. He keeps his car in there and supplies. He left the door unlocked every night."

Turner glanced over at the large man behind the counter, who looked like he was better suited to stepping into a ring of wrestlers than serving coffee. Bringing his gaze back to Emma, he said, "My mother taught us never to judge a book by its cover. I think she was talking about people like Gus and Sadie. No wonder they're special to you."

His quiet statement rocked Emma. He wasn't condemning her or feeling sorry for her. She'd expected one or the other responses, maybe both.

"Damn you," she muttered.

This time he was surprised. "Why?"

"You were supposed to be horrified and go running out of here as though you were afraid some of the grime of my life might rub off on you."

"Gee, Emma, you certainly have a great opinion of me," he drawled. "You make me sound like some goody-two-shoes yuppie with all the sensitivity of a razor blade."

Emma didn't realize until then that she'd been clinging to his hands as she told her story. His fingers were interwoven with hers, but not tightly. She could pull her hands away from his at any time. She realized the way he was holding her hands was more intimate and compelling because he wasn't forcing his strength on her. The hold he had on her heart was all the more powerful because he was giving her the opportunity to make her own choice.

She sighed heavily, her fingers tightening their grip. "What am I going to do with you, Turner?"

He grinned. "I could make a few suggestions."

"So could I. It would make things much easier if you threw me over your shoulder and took me home with you."

"Sorry. The caveman style isn't the way I want to get you into my bed. You're going to have to make the decision all on your own. We'll be together because you want to be in my bed, because you need to know what it would be like, because you want to be with me and no one else."

Emma wished she could read his mind as easily as he seemed to be able to read hers. Was his desire purely physical? Was that enough for him? Telling him about her past hadn't changed his mind about wanting to have an affair with her. But then why should it? It wasn't necessary for him to require references and a case history for a temporary relationship.

She pulled her hands away from his and slid across the seat to stand. Turner shifted, so he was facing her, his arm across the back of the booth. He made no move to leave the booth, even though he had to know touching her would turn her decision in his direction.

"I don't want to leave my car here," she said.

His eyes searched hers intently, and he understood what she was really saying. "I'll follow you home."

She nodded abruptly and was about to turn away to leave the diner when he said her name. Stopping midstep, she glanced at him over her shoulder.

"Are you sure?"

He was giving her a chance to change her mind, but it was too late. "I'm not sure this is the smartest thing I've ever done, nor am I sure I won't disappoint you, but I am sure I can't go another night without doing something about this aching emptiness I've had inside me since I met you."

Stunned by her honesty, Turner stood in front of her and ran his fingers along her jawline. She shuddered under his touch, and he wasn't at all surprised to see his own hand was shaking.

Threading his fingers through hers, he walked with her out of the diner to her car. It was more difficult than anything he'd ever done to let go of her hand so she could get in her car.

Before she started the engine, he leaned down and spoke through the window she'd rolled down. "Drive carefully," he said, his voice husky. "I wouldn't want anything to happen to you."

She met his intense gaze. "It already has."

Eight

Emma had no idea how she managed to drive home. Sadie had often said that the good Lord looked after drunks and fools. Emma qualified for the latter that night since her mind definitely was not on her driving.

Her thoughts were entirely on the man behind the wheel of the black Porsche following her. She wondered what he was thinking about, whether he was having the same misgivings as she was about her decision. Probably not, she decided. He was finally getting what he wanted, which, amazingly enough, was her.

All Turner would lose would be a few hours of sleep. She was giving up a great deal more, herself in exchange for a night of lovemaking. She would be making love. Turner would be having sex.

Pulling into her driveway, she shoved her doubts away, at least for the night. Lord knows they would come flooding back in the morning, but for now she would grasp at a few hours of being with the man she loved. It would be enough. It would have to be enough. It was all she was going to have.

One of the things she'd discovered living on the

streets was to make her own happiness, because it wasn't going to be given to her by anyone else. A major lesson was not to expect too much, then she wouldn't be disappointed.

Dragon jumped up and down in her usual ecstatic greeting the moment Emma opened her front door. The dog was easily placated by a few pats on the head before racing to the back door with a silent urgent request to be let outside.

Turner followed Emma into the kitchen and, like her, didn't turn the overhead light on. He leaned against the door frame and watched her lock the back door after she'd let the dog out.

"Will Dragon be staying outside the rest of the night?" he asked.

Emma turned, but remained at the back door. The light from the living room was behind him, and she couldn't read his expression in the darkened room.

"She will tonight."

Turner smiled slowly. "Are you going to stay by the back door until it's time to let her back in at dawn?"

She took one step forward, then another, removing her tweed jacket as she walked toward him. Keeping her gaze on his face, she tossed the jacket toward one of the chairs.

"Is it just me," she murmured, "or is it warm in here?"

The sound of slippery fabric sliding together seemed to vibrate through the silence as Turner took off his jacket. It fell on top of hers after a quick flick of his wrist sent it flying.

"It's bound to get hotter." He stood in the doorway, his hands on his hips. "You make me burn, Emma. You have since the first day you came to work. Sometimes all I had to do was hear your voice, and it was like a flash fire going through my veins."

"You hid it well. I thought you couldn't stand me."

She was closer. Another two steps and she would be in his arms. "I gave up trying to do anything about being attracted to you. You weren't exactly falling over yourself to be friendly."

She took one more step and stopped. "If I had wanted to be more friendly toward you, what would you have liked me to do?"

"Touch me."

She lifted her hand and laid her palm on his chest. "Like this?"

"That's my shirt. I want you to touch me."

Bringing up her other hand, she began to unbutton his shirt. After the last button was released, she raised her lashes slowly and met his gaze as she slid her hands under the cloth.

Turner sucked in his breath. Her soft hands flowed over his chest like electrified silk, sending shock waves through him. When the tip of one of her fingers brushed over a nipple, he couldn't stop the groan of pleasure that welled up inside him.

Emma misunderstood the cause of his reaction and froze. "Is it your ulcer?" She started to retreat from him, her eyes wide with concern. "I'm sorry, Turner. I completely forgot about your ulcer."

"Forget my ulcer." His hands clasped her upper arms, and he drew her into his arms. "Forget everything but me."

He brought his mouth down on hers with all the desperation and hunger he'd felt for her for too long. She opened up her heart and parted her lips to take him inside. She was vaguely aware of his strong thigh insinuating itself between her legs as his tongue surged between her teeth.

The familiar room seemed to spin around, and she clung to Turner, gasping breathlessly when he lifted his thigh against her. She arched her back and tightened her legs to hold him where her body throbbed and ached.

Turner broke away from her mouth and buried his lips against her throat. He was trembling as though he were suffering from a fever, his control almost nonexistent.

He claimed her mouth again and again, needing the taste of her, the closeness, the intimacy. The simple act of kissing a woman shouldn't make him feel so much, so damn good, but kissing Emma was like nothing he'd ever experienced before.

Even when he lifted her into his arms and carried her toward the stairs, he couldn't stop kissing her.

By some miracle, he managed the stairs without tumbling them both down into a heap at the bottom. His breathing was as ragged as his heartbeat when he pushed her bedroom door open with his shoulder. In three strides, he reached her bed and lowered her onto the blue-and-gold spread.

His hands went to his belt as he stood beside the bed looking down at her. Enough dim light from a street lamp shone into the room for him to see the blatant need glimmering in her eyes.

And a glimpse of a haunting sadness.

He dropped his hands and sat down on the edge of the bed near her hip. "Have you changed your mind?"

"No," she said unsteadily. "Have you?"

He slid his fingers through her hair, which was fanned out over the pillow. Somewhere between the kitchen and the bedroom, she'd lost the handkerchief securing her hair at the back of her neck. Her hair was as soft as silk and clung to his fingers.

"I haven't changed my mind," he said. "I want you even more than I did a few minutes ago, and I didn't think that was possible."

"I hear a but in there somewhere."

"Did Sadie ever warn you that men can be selfish as sin when they're aroused? I don't want to take anything from you you're not ready to give."

She wrapped her fingers around his wrist. "I know the facts of life. I lived in a variety of communes until I was eleven, Turner. It's impossible not to learn a great deal about human nature and human behavior when you all live, eat, and sleep as a community. The people who were members called themselves naturalists, which roughly meant they believed in doing what to them was natural. There were no legal marriages, but I learned early why there were so many children in the communes. They believed in free love with as many partners as they wanted."

His face was set in stark lines. "You weren't abused, were you?"

"I'm technically not a virgin due to a nasty fall off a roof, but I've never been with a man, if that's what you're asking. That doesn't mean I don't know what's going to happen." She sighed dramatically.

"Or what was going to happen before you suddenly got a conscience."

Her disgruntled tone of voice made him smile. "Emma?"

She frowned at him, wondering what other topic he wanted to cover when the last thing she felt like doing was talking.

"What?"

He stretched out beside her, slipping one of his legs between hers. "Why don't you shut up so I can kiss you?"

"Me? You were the one—"

He took full advantage of her open mouth, drawing her down with him into the turbulent sea of passion. Any remaining doubts he had were swept away, along with her clothing, then his. He was immensely pleased to find wisps of lace and silk under the serviceable denim jeans and cotton shirt. As much as he liked the sensual scraps of material, he didn't waste a second in removing them. He wanted nothing between them, not even the air they breathed.

"Lord, Emma," he rasped against one of the breasts he'd bared. "You're going to drive me out of my mind."

She stroked her hands over his back, reveling in the heat and strength under her fingers. There wasn't time to be self-conscious or to worry that she might not be capable of satisfying him. All she could do was writhe against him as she searched for the end to the tension coiling tighter and tighter within her. Instinctively she knew only Turner could provide the release.

His strong magical hands swept over her, leaving a trail of sensitized skin wherever he touched. When he slid his hand up her thigh and parted her moist heat, she arched her back and cried out.

"Emma," he groaned against her throat, then her mouth. He couldn't touch enough, feel enough, experience enough of her. He wanted more when he knew there couldn't possibly be more. Then he discovered there was when she slid her hand down between them and touched him.

Unable to hold out against the need to make her his, he slid his hands under her, cupping his fingers over her shoulders while his elbows took some of his weight off her. Savoring the delicious feel of her breasts against his chest, he tried to rein in his desperate need to sink his aching body into hers.

As he parted her legs and settled between them, she slowly opened her eyes and met his hot gaze. The wariness, the sadness was gone, replaced by a dazed desire.

"Put your arms around me, Emma," he ordered, surprised he could manage the simple act of speaking when he felt so full of so many emotions. "Hold me. I feel like I'm going to splinter into a million pieces."

Emma stroked her fingers through his hair, over his shoulders, down his spine. Nothing she'd ever felt was as strong, as warm, as powerful as his body.

She heard a note of awe in her voice when she whispered, "I've never felt this alive."

"Emma," he muttered against her throat. "I can't wait any longer. Don't let go of me. Stay with me the whole way."

Her answer was a movement of her hips, an invitation she wasn't aware she was issuing in her search for a closeness she was afraid was out of reach.

With a moan of surrender, Turner eased into her, sweat coating his skin from the control he had to exert so he wouldn't claim her with all the urgency his need was demanding. He was rewarded with a gasp of surprise that turned into a moan of pleasure as he forged deeply into her.

Emma was aware of the conflicting feelings of being helpless, yet stronger than she'd ever felt. She simply gave in to the stunning pleasure flowing from Turner to her, then back again. She heard her name as though he were calling her from a great distance and followed Turner over the edge.

When Emma slowly opened her eyes, she saw sunshine pouring through the window in her bedroom. Usually she closed the drapes so she wouldn't be assaulted by dawn's early light. She buried her face in the pillow to shut out the offending brightness, and her heart nearly stopped when a familiar scent clouded her mind.

The night in Turner's arms, the passion, the closeness, the incredible perfection all came rushing back.

She rolled over and searched the room, then listened for any sound of activity coming from the adjoining bathroom. All she heard was a familiar drone of snoring coming from the foot of the bed. Raising her head, she saw Dragon curled up near her feet.

Some of the glow warming her body dissolved

as she realized Turner had let her dog inside the house before he'd left. Without waking her, without a word of when he'd see her again, without even a casual thanks for the use of her bed and body.

If this was how one-night stands were usually conducted, Emma didn't think much of the rules.

She tossed the covers aside and walked barefoot across the carpeted floor to the closet, where she took a short terry robe off the hanger. After tying the sash, she opened a drawer in the bureau and gathered up clean underwear. Clutching the lacy lingerie in one hand and rubbing her sleepy eyes with the other, she walked groggily to the bathroom. Leaning her hands on the sink, she steeled herself to look at her reflection.

A piece of paper was in her way, stuck on the mirror with a Band-Aid.

She peeled the paper off the mirror and read Turner's familiar handwriting:

Checked on Audrey at seven o'clock. She's okay. Fed Dragon. (Used the last can of dog food.) Stay home today and work on your book. I'll be in San Francisco all day. Will be back at seven tonight to take you out to dinner. (Wear the green dress I saw hanging in your closet.)

Still holding the note in her hand, Emma sank down on the cold rim of the porcelain bathtub. Aside from the fact that Turner's note read like an office memo, she no longer felt hurt and humiliated. She couldn't even take exception to the series of orders he'd written down, even though out of principle she probably should.

Knowing that he planned to see her again helped her face the day without any regrets. She expected to have them eventually when he was gone for good. Until that time she would enjoy what she could have for as long as possible.

The day at home flew by faster than she'd expected, even without the hustle and bustle of deadlines and schedules, ringing telephones, and the endless research that never ended but only changed topics. With Dragon keeping her company, she spent most of the day in her studio working on her drawings. And listening for the phone. She wasn't expecting Turner to call, but when she'd run over to see Audrey earlier that morning, the expectant mother had complained of a backache and feeling as edgy as a bird walking on a hot wire. Since Emma was going to be home all day and Audrey planned to rest, Emma didn't bother phoning her neighbor every hour. Audrey was to call her if she needed anything.

A little after six that evening, Emma had already taken a shower and had gotten as far as putting on the green slip that went under the dress Turner had asked her to wear, when the phone rang. As she crossed the bedroom to the table beside her bed, she hated the insecurity that had her wondering if Turner was calling to cancel their evening.

Instead of Turner's deep voice, she heard Audrey yelling her name. "I'm here," she said. "Calm down, Audrey. Is it the baby?"

In between panting breaths, Audrey snapped,

"Well, if it isn't, it's a hell of a rehearsal for the real thing."

"I'll be right there."

"That's what I was hoping you'd say." She made a sound of distress that tapered off into an urgent plea. "You might want to move it along. My water just broke."

Emma's stomach did a double somersault. "Hang on, Audrey. I'm coming."

Shoving her feet into the green pumps she'd removed from their box earlier, she grabbed her trench coat out of the closet with such force, the hanger fell onto the floor. She fastened the belt around her waist as she ran down the stairs, grabbing her purse and her car keys from the table near the door. Ignoring Dragon, who had gotten into the spirit of things by running around the living room with her favorite teddy bear in her mouth, Emma snapped the lock on the door and slammed it shut behind her.

By the time she'd backed her car out of the garage, Audrey was slowly and carefully descending the steps of her front porch, as though she were walking on eggs. She had one hand on her stomach and the other on the small of her back. Leaving the engine running, Emma rushed around the front of the car to assist Audrey into the front seat. After managing to fasten the seat belt over Audrey's sizable stomach, she raced back to Audrey's porch to retrieve the overnight case just inside the door. So far everything was going according to their carefully mapped out plan.

"Did you call the doctor?" she asked as she slid into the driver's seat.

"Yes," Audrey gasped.

Backing out of her driveway, Emma almost ran over her mailbox when Audrey let out a sound that sent shivers down her spine.

"Breathe, Audrey. Remember the Lamaze class? Do the breathing exercises."

"I would be more than happy to breathe," Audrey panted, holding her stomach with both hands, "except for the minor complication of this child doing a tap dance with cleats on."

Emma kept her eyes on the road and her foot pressed down on the accelerator. "You can have a chat with him about his manners after he's born."

After another episode of gritting her teeth and doing her breathing exercises, Audrey closed her eyes. "Talk to me. It'll take my mind off the pain. Tell me about your love life with the lawyer."

Taking her gaze off the road long enough to check the time of Audrey's latest contraction, she chuckled. "I don't remember a discussion of my personal life being included in the instructions at Lamaze class."

"It should be. Hearing the juicy details of your romance with tall, dark, and lethal will keep my mind off the movie the Lamaze instructor had us watch on childbirth. And don't tell me there are no juicy details. I heard his car start up at five-thirty this morning. I happened to be awake, taking one of the four hundred trips to the bathroom I make every night. If he was at your house till the wee hours of the morning, I doubt it was because you were playing a hot game of canasta."

Emma honked impatiently at the car ahead of them when it didn't respond quickly enough to the light turning green. The driver made a rude gesture but moved. Audrey giggled and Emma joined her.

After timing another contraction, Emma took several deep breaths herself to calm down. Audrey's labor was progressing a little too fast for her peace of mind, and she was having visions of delivering a baby by the side of the road.

Because she needed to take her mind off the miles yet to travel to the hospital, she said, "Turner met Sadie last night at Gus's diner."

Audrey's eyes widened as she turned her head to look at Emma. "Well, that's moving things right along. You've never taken a guy to meet the family before."

"I didn't take him this time. You sent him after me, remember?"

"Oh," Audrey breathed. "So I did. So what happened? Since his car was in your driveway most of the night, Sadie evidently didn't scare him away."

"Not that Sadie didn't try," Emma said wryly. "If Turner's occupation was anything other than lawyer, Sadie might have been a little more cordial." The lights of the hospital were just ahead. "He didn't seem overly shocked to learn about my past, about my living on the streets. Maybe after he has time to think about it, he'll realize we aren't suited for each other, but until then, I'm going to enjoy our relationship as long as I can."

Audrey was about to argue against Emma's thinking when another wave of pain clawed its way through her body. Perspiration coated her skin and her breathing grew uneven.

Emma was never so glad to see the outline of San Jose General Hospital in all her life. From the moment she dispatched Audrey to the maternity floor, the next four hours were unlike anything she'd ever experienced. The Lamaze training had prepared her for the technical procedure of birth, but she hadn't expected to feel both tearful and elated when Audrey's little girl was born.

After mother and child had been checked over and pronounced in terrific shape, Emma found her coat at the nurses' station and removed the hospital gown she'd worn in the delivery room. The unexpected sound of several wolf whistles had her looking down at herself. She'd forgotten that all she had on was the green slip and little else.

The reason she had the slip on in the first place came flooding back to her as she yanked the coat on. Turner had planned to pick her up at seven o'clock to go out to dinner. She glanced at the large round clock on the wall. Four hours ago.

She wondered if he'd be angry that he'd been stood up, or if he'd shrug it off as just one of those things.

Before she left the hospital, she had one more thing to do. She put through a call to the dispatcher of the trucking firm where Audrey's husband worked and asked them to give Dory Twosteps a message on his radio. She smiled at the excited voice on the other end of the phone when she related the news that Dory had a little girl, then hung up the phone, her smile fading.

Envy was an emotion she had learned to control over the years. Wanting something someone else had was useless and a waste of time. But it was the only explanation for her desire to have what Audrey had; a husband who adored her, a healthy baby, and an extensive family on both sides that often filled the Twostepses' backyard for cookouts.

She drove considerably more slowly back to her house than she had when she'd left with Audrey. After all the noise, commotion, and strain of the past four hours, she was feeling oddly depressed and not looking forward to returning to her empty home.

The first thing she noticed when she turned into the cul-de-sac was the black Porsche parked in her driveway. Her headlights picked out the shape of a man slumped in the front seat as she stopped her car a couple of feet from Turner's bumper. Cutting off the lights and the engine, she got out. It took a few seconds for her eyes to adjust to the dim light coming from the street lamp in front of her house.

Approaching his car, Emma saw that Turner was sound asleep. For a minute she let herself enjoy the sight of him before she opened the car door and reached in to shake his shoulder.

"Turner! Wake up."

His hand reacted first. Long, strong fingers tightened around her wrist. His warm breath caressed her hand when he kissed her palm. Then he opened his eyes and gave her a lopsided smile.

"Are you okay?" he asked, his voice husky with sleep.

"I'm fine. Why are you sitting out here?"

"We have a date." He stretched, then levered his cramped body out of the front seat. Towering over her, he looked down at her and asked again, "Are you sure you're all right?"

"I'm sure."

The deceptive calm in his voice changed to a

whiplash accusation. "Then where the hell have you been? I've been half out of my mind worrying about you, you idiotic woman. I had visions of you in a wreck somewhere, hurt, unconscious, and bleeding."

Startled by the abrupt change in mood, she asked, "Why would you think that?"

He leaned down until his nose was only inches away from hers. "Because that would explain why you never tried to phone me and let me know why you weren't waiting for me when I arrived. You have my office number, my car number, my home phone number, and you know how to reach me on my pager. Linda could have given you the number of the office in San Francisco, where I had a meeting. Hell, except for the short time I left the pager in my briefcase when I went to the men's room, I could be reached every second of the day. I figured if you were able to talk, you would have contacted me."

After the dispiriting ride home, his bad-tempered tirade was music to her ears. He wasn't spouting off because his ego had been bruised when she stood him up. He'd been honestly worried about her. That felt good. In fact, it felt terrific.

"Everything kind of happened at once," she said. "Audrey called as I was getting dressed around six-thirty and said it was time to go to the hospital. Things got a little hectic after that."

"Is she all right?"

"The last time I saw her, she and her new daughter were getting better acquainted."

"All right," he said. "I understand why you left. I just wish you'd have gotten in touch with me."

She slipped her arms around his neck and rose up on her toes. "Do you feel better now?"

"A little." His arms encircled her, and he buried his face in the soft curve of her neck. "Don't ever do that to me again, Emma. You scared the hell out of me."

"I doubt if such an occasion will occur in the near future. I'm all out of pregnant neighbors."

He raised his head and looked down at her, his fingers going to the belt of her coat. "You can make it up to me," he murmured as he slid his hands inside her coat. Shock widened his eyes and he parted the front of her coat. "Good Lord, woman. Did you go to the hospital like this?"

"I told you things got a little hectic. I didn't take the time to finish getting dressed when Audrey said it was time to go."

With one smooth movement, Turner lifted her off her feet and started walking toward the house. "I can see we're going to have to have a little talk about you driving around San Jose half-naked."

Her arms wound around his neck. "You're going to give me a long lecture now?"

His eyes glimmered with heat. "Later."

Nine

If someone had asked Emma to describe how her life had changed almost overnight, she wouldn't have been able to choose only one word. There were too many that applied, like perfect, enchanting, fantasylike, exciting. Every romantic dream she'd ever had as a teenager had magically come true.

Except her knight in shining armor drove a black Porsche and wore a business suit during the day and more casual attire, usually jeans, in the evening.

Emma never knew what to expect with Turner, which she admitted was part of the attraction. On Friday night he took her to a quiet restaurant for dinner, then they finished the evening with a visit to the Japanese Tea Gardens, where they fed the koi fish and walked along the lantern-lighted paths. Somehow he had arranged for the use of the teahouse after hours, and they watched a kimono-clad woman gracefully enacting the elaborate ancient tea ceremony.

Lunch on Saturday consisted of a couple of hours of debauchery at an ice-cream parlor, where they shared an enormous concoction of different-flavored ice cream, whipped cream, and toppings. Turner told her of several incidents of mutual terrorizing between his brothers and his sister while she let him see glimpses of the unusual world that had been hers when she was a child.

After lunch he went with her to Eastridge Mall, where they wandered into various shops that featured infant clothing and supplies, helping her look for the right present to purchase for Audrey's daughter. It took nearly two hours, and to Turner's amazement, he wasn't bored one single minute. He'd never spent that much time in a mall in his life, but with Emma, it was fun sorting through all the tiny clothes, playing music boxes, and trying to guess what some of the display items were used for.

Turner had enjoyed his first full day off in weeks so much, he hadn't left himself much time to go to his apartment to change before taking Emma out for the evening. He had managed to get tickets to see *Showboat* at the Circle Theatre.

In the rush to change and return for Emma, he forgot the tickets in his apartment. When he picked up Emma, he told her they had to go back to his place to get the tickets. This was as good a time as any for her to see his apartment, he decided. If she was still willing to go on seeing him after having proof he had the decorating taste of a slug, he would know she had to care for him.

At his apartment he unlocked his door and ushered her inside. Emma took three steps into the living room, then stopped to stare at the walls, the carpet, the furnishings. Practically everything in the room was a strange gray green that wasn't on any color wheel she'd ever seen.

Turner picked up the forgotten tickets from the long narrow table in the entrance hall, which someone had attempted to paint to look like marble and hadn't succeeded. The legs of the table looked like they had a bad case of varicose veins.

"Well?" he asked when she didn't say anything.

"Well, what?" She brought her gaze back to the only object in the whole room that didn't offend her eyes. Turner.

"No pithy comments about my lack of taste? My sister's first reaction was to tell me my apartment reminded her of pond scum."

Emma glanced at the five-seat sectional in dark moss green that stretched and curved around the walls. "That about says it all," she said. "Lord, Turner. I'd have nightmares if this color was the last thing I saw when I shut my eyes."

He walked over to her, smiling. "I'll just have to make sure I'm the last sight you see before you close your eyes if we spend the night here."

Emma knew that would do it. Whenever she was in his arms, she forgot about everything but him. When he touched her, the world disappeared.

She had the proof that happened when he lowered his head to kiss her. The moment his mouth covered hers, she was immersed in desire that swirled, tugged, and drew her deeper into its depths, until she was drowning in a sensual whirlpool.

With a muttered oath, he raised his head but didn't release his tight hold on her. "If we don't leave now, we're going to miss the play."

"What play?" she murmured against his throat.

Chuckling, he held her a few moments longer. "I had plans to dazzle you with an evening of culture by taking you to see *Showboat* at the Circle Theatre. If we don't leave now, we'll miss the first act."

He kissed her again, then released her. Taking her hand, he drew her toward the front door. "I might not be the most romantic knight around, but even I draw the line at making love to you in a place that would give you nightmares afterward."

Emma disagreed. He was the most romantic knight she'd ever known or had even dreamed would ever be in her life. The glorious nights with Turner had opened her to an intimacy she couldn't have imagined before, a closeness she savored every minute they were together. She felt she'd finally caught the brass ring of happiness, and she was going to hold on to it as tightly as she could until fate forced her to hand it back.

And she had no illusions that that day would come. She had never been taught to believe in Santa Claus, the Easter Bunny, or the Tooth Fairy. She'd been raised by people who taught that nature would take its course, whether it brought flash floods or days full of sunshine. She didn't adhere to most of their teachings, but she did believe that Fate could be a fickle lady. She could read every book in the universe, believe that hard work would be rewarded, but she was also a realist.

The only happily-ever-afters occurred in fairy tales.

Throughout the weekend she noticed moments when Turner became unusually quiet and introspective, as though he was preoccupied with thoughts he didn't want to share with her. Then those moments would pass and he would be back with her totally. She told herself not to mind that he was keeping things from her. As a rule, she preferred to know where she was going in her life and how she was going to get there. With Turner, that wasn't an option. She had to take their relationship an hour at a time.

If he never once mentioned how he felt about her during the intimate hours they spent in her bed, she tried to tell herself it was enough that she loved him, that he was there with her at that moment.

Never once did she ever let it slip how she felt about him.

Her previous life had forced her to form a core of reticence deep inside her. Yet she'd told Turner more about herself than she normally confided to people. Never once did he abuse the trust she'd put in him. In turn, she discovered he had his own private corners he didn't invite her to see. He gave her freely of his passion, his desire, and his body. His innermost feelings, however, remained his alone.

Especially about his ability to draw.

After being turned down abruptly when she asked him Friday evening to give his opinion of a painting she was working on, she never asked again. Still, she couldn't understand why Turner continued to reject his artistic nature. She'd observed too many indications of how talented he was and had seen the look of anguish mixed with longing in his eyes the day he'd corrected the little boy's expression.

Sunday afternoon after they returned from a late brunch, Emma could no longer fool herself that they could go on as they had the last couple of days. Turner had barely said two words during the drive back to her house. Instead of a comfortable silence between them, the air seemed to crackle with a current of tension that emanated from Turner.

When he parked in her driveway and made no immediate move to get out of the car, she waited for him to say he wouldn't be staying the night with her.

He finally opened his door and got out. A feeling of dread settled like a lead weight in Emma's stomach as she walked beside him toward her front door. He didn't leave her at the front door as she'd expected, though. He held out his hand for her key and unlocked the door. She walked into her house slowly, fearing every second she'd be called back so Turner could tell her he wasn't staying.

Dragon demanded her usual pat on the head, which she received from both Turner and Emma, although not with their usual enthusiasm. The dog accepted the abstracted strokes as her due, then dashed toward the kitchen door to be let out.

When Emma went to open the door for Dragon, she left Turner standing in front of the window in the living room. He was still there when she returned. He was deep in thought, staring out at the quiet cul-de-sac. She didn't ask him what was wrong, although it was obvious something was.

One of the things Sadie had taught Emma was to face a problem rather than ignore it and hope it would go away. Sadie had said trouble usually stuck around unless someone gave it a swift kick in the rear. The older woman had always encouraged Emma to block trouble or beat the tar out of it, rather than let it beat her down.

And it wasn't in Emma's nature to prolong agony by waiting for it. If she was due to receive some bad news, she wanted to hear it now, not wonder what disaster lay ahead of her.

Fear clawed at her insides with sharp talons as she gazed at Turner's back, but she refused to give in to it. If Turner was going to break the fragile bond that had been growing between them, she wanted the killing stroke to be quick and merciful.

Leaning one hand on the back of the rocking chair, she took off first one of her loafers, then the other. She held one directly in front of her. And dropped it. The thudding sound the shoe made as it hit the floor was magnified by the stifling silence in the room.

Turner jerked his head around, a frown appearing between his brows. He looked at her, then at the shoe on the floor.

"What are you doing?" he asked.

"Waiting for the other shoe to drop."

He shifted his gaze to the shoe in her hand, then back down at the one on the floor. "Is this some new parlor game?"

"It's no game," she said, wondering how big a fool she would make of herself before the evening was over. She was also amazed to realize a tiny flicker of hope was valiantly striving to stay alive inside her. "Why don't you just get it over with, Turner? You don't need to worry that I'm going to create a scene or fall apart. I've been expecting this."

"Expecting what?" Thoroughly confused, he asked, "What are you talking about? Get what over with?"

"The other shoe dropping." She held the other loafer at arm's length and let it fall to the floor beside the other one. "The farewell speech."

He rubbed his forehead with his fingers. "I thought you and I were on the same wavelength, but you apparently switched channels on me. Who's supposed to be making a farewell speech?"

"You are."

"I'm supposed to be saying good-bye to you?"

"Yes."

"Why?"

His questions were only drawing out the difficult ending, she thought with frustration. Her gaze shifted to the books on the shelves. "None of my books deals with ending a relationship, so I don't know if I'm doing my part correctly. I have no way of knowing how the other women you've been involved with have reacted when you're no longer interested in them. You'll have to let me know if there's something I should be saying or doing."

"There haven't been all that many," he replied. "Am I supposed to understand the connection between you dropping your shoes and the other women I've known?"

"They were temporary, and so am I. I'm not sure what the usual procedure is. All I can do is react in my own way, which is to open the door and let you go." She walked over to the front door and turned the knob. "There won't be any recriminations, tears, or pleading with you to change your mind, if that's why you're delaying telling me our relationship is over. You're free to leave whenever you want."

Turner finally saw a glimmer of light through the fog of confusion. He wasn't going anywhere, but for some ridiculous reason that's exactly what Emma was expecting.

"What makes you think I want to end our relationship?"

"You have a habit of fiddling with your watch when you have something unpleasant to do, like tell a client you won't take their case. Or when you were trying to figure out a way to tell Mrs. Kimball you hated that black leather contemporary chair she bought for your office." Her gaze lowered to his wrist, where his fingers were playing with the watchband. "That and the fact you haven't said more than seven words since we finished brunch, and those were, *Are you ready?* and *Do you have everything?*"

Raising one eyebrow, he smiled. "Do you usually count every word I say?"

"You're changing the subject," she said crossly, seeing nothing amusing about this situation.

"That's kind of hard for me to do, Emma, when I haven't the faintest notion what the subject is. You lost me when you dropped the first shoe."

"I'm trying to tell you that I'll understand if you have something else you'd rather do tonight. I don't expect you to spend every minute of your free time with me. All you have to do is say so, Turner. The door is open."

"Close it."

She bit her lip, then asked, "With you on the inside or the outside?"

He was amused by her choice of words, but he knew she wouldn't appreciate his humor at this particular moment. He definitely intended to be inside her before morning. Several times.

Unless she was serious about wanting him to leave, he reflected. His healing ulcer sent a warning twinge that reminded him of what stress could do to him. Even thinking of living without Emma caused him more pain than any ulcer ever could.

"Maybe I should be asking you the same question, Emma. Have you been having second thoughts about us? Do you want me to leave and never come back?"

The prospect of never seeing him again tightened her throat, and she was unable to say even one word. She shook her head instead, saying more with the stricken expression in her eyes than any words could have conveyed.

"Just because I'm fiddling with my watch, you take it to mean I'm tired of our relationship?" He closed the distance between them and framed her face with his hands, not at all surprised to realize she was trembling. His hands weren't that steady either.

Emma was usually so self-contained, but not when she thought they were breaking up. He liked knowing she didn't take their relationship lightly. If she was any other woman, she might have thrown her shoes at him rather than simply dropping them to make a point.

And he would have walked out the door if any other woman had started pushing for a commitment. Hell, he would have run as fast as he could.

That was before Emma.

"For an intelligent woman, you're using incredibly dumb logic. I admit I have something on my mind, but it has nothing to do with walking out your door until morning."

Relief made her feel almost light-headed. Their time together would not end tonight.

She sighed deeply. "I suppose everyone's entitled to make a fool of themselves once in a while. Tonight it's my turn."

His lips brushed over hers. "I like knowing it would bother you if you didn't see me again. It would bother the hell out of me too."

He felt her hands at his waist, her fingers tightening when he kissed her deeply. He would have been more than content to continue kissing her knowing where that would lead, but the clock that had been ticking in his head reminded him that he was running out of time.

Breaking away from her mouth, he buried his face in her hair and cursed under his breath. "I wish I'd given my father a tie for his birthday instead of that damned fax machine."

Emma made a choking sound that sounded like a giggle cut off in the middle. "Now who isn't making any sense?"

Loosening his hold on her, Turner ran his hand down her arm until he found her hand. He walked over to the couch, drawing her along with him. "Come and sit down. This might take a while."

His heavier weight on the cushion had her leaning toward him, and he took full advantage of that by holding her close to his side.

"Do you remember me telling you about the Camelot chess set?" he asked.

"Of course. Willoughby Knight sculpted it, and it's been in your family for decades. What's that got to do with a fax machine?"

"I gave my father a fax machine for his birthday last month, and I could paper my office with the letters he's been sending. Not just to me. Michael, Ryder, and Silver have been getting almost daily demands from King to stop playing around and get busy making babies. He wants to become a grandfather and nothing any of us has said has changed his mind."

Emma would have given a great deal to know exactly what Turner's reply to his father had been. "I don't know your father, but you aren't the type to let someone nag or persuade you into doing something you don't want to do."

"If that's true, why have I been eating omelets instead of pizza and vegetable casseroles instead of a thick, juicy steak? Why am I spending my evenings with you instead of working? You even changed the coffee at the office to decaf. What's that if it isn't persuading me to change my ways?"

"You wouldn't do any of those things if you didn't want to, Turner. Even if I have tried to steer you toward a healthier life-style, that's a lot different from telling you to get married and produce children."

He tipped her chin up so he could see her eyes. "I saw your face when you were holding Audrey's baby this morning. Have you ever thought about having a child?"

Emma grasped his wrist to remove his hand. "You're changing the subject. You were going to tell me about your father's latest request."

"King's last letter was not primarily to remind me of my duty to provide him with grandchildren. Although he managed to work in a reminder that I wasn't getting any younger and neither is he. No, the letter was about the chess set."

Emma shoved aside the thought of carrying a child fathered by Turner, although it wasn't easy. "What about the chess set?"

"He said he wants to sell it." In a few sentences, Turner told her about the locking mechanism securing the gold set in its glass case. "Without all of our shields in place, King can't remove the Camelot set. He's asked me to bring mine on Monday. Michael arrived early last week. I haven't been able to get in touch with Ryder. His answering service said he's still in Texas, so he hasn't been summoned to England yet. He's probably out searching for an oil well somewhere and hasn't checked his messages lately. According to Michael, Silver's in Kentucky at the headquarters of Knight Enterprises, taking care of some business for King. I haven't been able to reach her."

"They wouldn't agree to sell the set either, would they?"

He shook his head, then turned to look at her as he realized she had automatically included him in the refusal to sell the Camelot set. "I didn't say I wasn't going to agree to sell the set."

"Tradition and family mean too much for you to give up a family treasure."

He lifted her onto his lap so he could see her better. And hold her. "Now what makes you think you know me so well that you can determine that? The money King would get for the chess set would be one hell of a sizable inheritance even divided four ways."

"I've heard your voice when you talk about your family, even your father when he's driving you nuts, and I saw the pride and love in your eyes when you told me about your mother climbing up into the tree house you and your brother built. I also know that money doesn't mean that much to you. The work you do at Kimball and Knight is for the challenge, not for the fees you collect."

He ran his hand over her thigh. "It's a little scary that you know me so well, Emma. I thought a bit of mystery was supposed to be good for a relationship."

Her gaze searched his. "It depends on what type of relationship you want."

The odd, defensive note in her voice stilled his hand. "What kind of relationship do you think we have?"

She laid her hand over his heart, where she could feel his accelerated heartbeat. "Definitely a physical one."

She was right in her assessment as far as she went, Turner thought. She just hadn't gone far enough. "And what else do we have between us? Friendship, trust, respect?"

"I'd like to think so." And more, so much more on her part, Emma thought as she reveled in the feel of his hard body so close to hers. He dropped his gaze to the front of her shirt, where his fingers were playing with the button between her breasts. "Has it ever occurred to you how much I know about you, how much trust you've given me, how much of yourself you've given me since we've become lovers?"

She knew. She hadn't realized he did too. Although she should have expected Turner to have arrived at those conclusions without any help from her. His ability to read people wasn't used only in the office or the courtroom.

"Are you concerned that I expect more from you than an affair?" she asked cautiously. "Is that what's been bothering you tonight? If it is, you don't need to worry about it. I'm not going to be one of those demanding women who insist you do the right thing by carting me off to the altar. I entered into this relationship with my eyes open."

He didn't look pleased that she'd let him off the hook of matrimony. In fact, he was scowling at her. "Then maybe you need stronger glasses."

"Why?"

He lifted her off his lap, setting her down on the couch. Standing, he took several steps away from her, then turned to face her. "Because you can't see that I care about you so much I've been half-crazy with the thought of losing you. I've been putting off making plans to go to England to see what my father is up to because I don't want to leave you even for a couple of days."

She stared at him as she picked out the astounding part of his statement. "You care about me?"

He scowled again. Obviously the astonishment in her voice didn't help soothe his temper. "Sadie has sadly neglected your education when it comes to men, Emma, if you think I could make love to you as often, as intently as I have just because I wanted sex with a woman. You're the only woman I want, and I don't want to go even a day without seeing you. I want you to come to England with me. King wants me to fly home tomorrow, but I'm going to put him off for a day or two. Come with me."

"To England?" she asked, dazed from everything he'd said during the last several minutes. In all the words she'd heard, good-bye hadn't been one of them.

Taking a deep calming breath, Turner returned to the couch and hunkered down in front of her with his hands on her thighs. "We're still too new to be separated right now, Emma. You aren't sure of me, of us yet, and I don't want to take the chance you'll conjure demons that don't exist if I leave for a few days. Come with me. I've met your family. Now I want you to meet mine, at least King and perhaps Michael, if he's still there. You can meet Ryder and Silver another time."

Emma lifted her hand and let her fingers linger over the silken strands of his hair. "I don't think that's a good idea."

"Why not? You'll be meeting them eventually. Why not start with King and Michael, then we'll get to Ryder and Silver later."

"Your family might not approve of my background," she said quietly. "Not everyone does, and I'm not going to lie about it if your father asks. I'm not ashamed of being raised by Sadie, but to most people, she's an eccentric bag lady who lives on the streets."

"You haven't seen eccentric until you've met King Knight," he said dryly. "I should be the one who's wary of having you meet my family, not the other way around." He enclosed her hands in his. "If you don't go, I'm not going either."

"You have to go. You need to find out why your father would want to sell something that means so much to your family."

He brought their joined hands up to his lips and brushed his mouth over hers. "You wouldn't want my ulcer to act up again, would you? I'm not supposed to have any stress, remember? I'll have a whole carload of stress if you don't come with me."

"That's not fair."

"All's fair in love and war," he said lightly, although the expression in his eyes was very serious.

"This isn't war."

He smiled. "Then I guess it must be love."

"That's not funny," she snapped, her voice cracking on the last word.

He met her eyes. "I'm not laughing, Emma. Evidently I'm serious."

Emma couldn't do a single thing to stop the tears from welling up in her eyes, his image blurring as she stared at him.

"Don't," he said roughly.

"I can't help it."

He cupped the side of her face and brushed away a single tear that escaped from the corner of her eye. "Tell me why you're crying. Would my loving you be so awful?"

"It would be wonderful if it was true."

"It is true. I love you. I think I've been in love with you from the first day you came to work for Kimball and Knight, but I was too stupid and too stubborn to admit it."

Through her tears, Emma searched his eyes and found what she was looking for. Throwing herself into his arms, she started crying in earnest.

Wrapping his arms around her, Turner let the momentum of her weight carry them both to the floor. His hands soothed, and he whispered sweet loving words to calm her, although neither would be able to remember what he said. Turner just knew he wanted her to stop crying. He'd never been very good at dealing with a woman's tears.

"You're going to have me bawling in a minute if you don't stop, sweetheart," he murmured. "I hope this isn't going to be your normal reaction whenever I tell you I love you. Now that I've got the hang of it, I plan on saying it a lot."

Emma sniffled indelicately and raised her head from his chest. She was beginning to believe he meant what he'd said. He was looking at her as though she was the most beautiful woman on earth, when she knew her eyes were red and her mascara was probably smeared. It had to be love.

Rubbing her hand across her lashes, she blinked several times so she could see him clearly. "I don't know why I'm crying. I never cry."

"For someone who's never done it before, you could win a championship." He brought his hands up to slide his fingers through her hair, holding her head so she had to continue looking at him. "I've never told another woman I love her, so I'm not an expert on how women react to a declaration of love. Somehow I expected a different reaction. Like you announcing how you feel about me."

It was the first time she'd ever heard a note of uncertainty in his voice, and she was stunned.

"The people who raised me in the communes spoke of loving their fellowman, loving the trees, the rocks, the birds, each other. Sadie likes to say she loves a good argument, the red suede boots I gave her for Christmas, and Gus's lasagne. The word is used a great deal, but I never really knew what the feeling of love was until I met you."

He looked at her with raw emotion darkening his eyes. "Lord, Emma. You fill me with so many emotions, I feel like I could drown in them."

She released several buttons on his shirt so she could slide her hands over his warm solid body. "All right," she whispered as she lowered her head to take a flat nipple into her mouth.

He shuddered. "What's all right?"

"For you to drown." She continued kissing him, leaving a moist trail wherever her lips touched him. When she reached his mouth, she looked into his eyes and added, "As long as you take me under with you."

He rolled her over and kissed her with a desperate hunger.

Ten

Emma barely had time to get accustomed to the astonishing fact that Turner loved her when he was whisking her off to get her picture taken for her passport. She had tried to use the lack of a valid birth certificate as an excuse not to accompany him to England, since she needed one in order to get a passport.

The thought of meeting King Knight was daunting, not only because he was a famous artist, but also because she was going to be uncomfortable tagging along with Turner. How would he introduce her? she couldn't help wondering. As his paralegal, his friend, his lover, his mistress? Any of those labels would be correct except for the last one, but they weren't the kind of descriptions she liked for their relationship.

She had been thrilled to hear him say he loved her, but she hadn't heard other words like forever, marriage, commitment. Maybe she never would hear those words, she thought as she blinked from the flash of the camera taking her photo.

She certainly wouldn't hear those important promises if Turner was in England and she was in San Jose.

Turner didn't want to use the forged birth certificate Sadie had provided Emma years ago. He made a few phone calls to several people, who in turn contacted other influential friends who could expedite legalities, and eventually a legal certificate validating Emma Valerian's existence was created. It was amazing what a little clout and special contacts in the judicial system could do in such a short time.

When Turner took the new copy off the fax machine in his office late Monday morning, he handed it to her. Emma held the document for a long time, reading it over and over. She couldn't explain the feeling of completion the birth certificate gave her. The piece of paper granted her a feeling of existence she'd never truly felt before.

She took a copy of the certificate with her when she left the office to go home to start packing.

Even with Turner's contacts, the necessary paperwork for Emma's passport was a tricky proposition. Still, he arranged to have the passport done up in a day. He and Emma could pick it up at the passport office in San Francisco before they left for England Tuesday morning.

As hard as he tried the rest of the day, Turner wasn't able to get much accomplished. He would have preferred spending the day with Emma rather than at his desk. The complete reversal of his priorities didn't escape him. Practicing law had been the most important thing in his life for years. And still was to some extent. Now that he had Emma in his life, though, he no longer felt his career was everything.

Emma had become as necessary as the air he breathed.

By six o'clock, he hung up the phone for the last time, called good night to Harry—who was back from New York—and left. As he waited for the elevator he realized he was hungry, not too surprising since he hadn't taken the time to eat lunch. His first impulse was to pick up a pizza on the way to Emma's. Since his ulcer and Emma would both object, he compromised on Chinese takeout.

Getting into the elevator, he smiled as he thought about spending the rest of the evening with Emma. He would make long, slow love to her until they were sated. Then he'd take her again.

He wasn't surprised to feel his body's reaction to the tantalizing thought of loving Emma long into the night. He'd reacted to her the same way for the last two years, and that was before he'd known the glorious sensations he would experience every time he became part of her.

The elevator seemed to be taking longer than usual to reach the ground floor. When it finally stopped, he hurried through the opened doors.

The one thing he could be thankful for was that his brothers weren't around to see him acting like a moony-eyed teenager. Or Silver. He knew exactly how they would react—they would tease him unmercifully, which was what he'd do to any of them if they were ever in the same condition.

Thinking of his siblings reminded him of the phone call he'd made to Knight's Keep that afternoon. He'd wanted to give his father his flight number and arrival time and to tell him he was bringing a guest. He'd ended up talking to his brother again. King still hadn't returned, Michael had said. As they talked Turner had begun to wonder if his brother had come down with the same malady King seemed to be suffering from, whatever it was. His older brother had sounded oddly distracted, as if the situation with the Camelot set was more of a nuisance than a real problem. Even more odd was that Michael didn't seem anxious to get back to his ranch. Michael usually acted as though the rails of his fences would fall down if he wasn't there.

Turner suddenly started to laugh when he realized why Michael wasn't eager to leave England. It had to be a woman. Only the female of the species could mess up relatively sane men's minds and change their priorities. If he was a betting man, Turner would put fifty bucks on his brother being struck by the same lightning bolt that had hit him.

Now Turner had three reasons to go to England: to introduce Emma to his father and brother, to find out what was going on with King wanting to sell the chess set, and to meet the woman who could make his brother think about something other than horses.

When he told Emma about his suspicions concerning Michael, Turner knew he'd have to put his brother's situation in a different way. Growing up with a sister had taught him that women thought differently about just about everything than men did. He knew Emma was nervous enough about meeting his family. He didn't need to give her the impression that he thought it amusing that his brother had finally met his match. Emma might not consider Michael falling for a woman to be as funny as he did.

Suddenly impatient to hear her voice, he punched out her home number on his car phone.

He heard the sound of the phone being picked up, then a rather frazzled feminine voice said, "What?"

"Are we having a bad day?" he asked with just the right amount of concern in his voice. Or so he thought.

"Turner, it's not funny." The extra time to get ready hadn't helped Emma at all. Whenever she thought about meeting Turner's father, she wished she could have a month. Maybe two. A year would be nice. "You know that list I made out last night of all the things I have to do before I leave?"

"Of course. We went over it together just before you seduced me—"

She cut him off. "Never mind. The purpose of the list was to mark off each item when it was done. But when I finish one, I think of two others that have to go on the list. I'm never going to be ready."

"Audrey's going to take care of Dragon and take in your mail, Dory will water your flowers and mow your lawn," he reminded her in a reasonable tone. "You left a message with Gus to tell Sadie why you wouldn't be seeing her for a week. It's no big deal if the rest doesn't get done. Just throw a few of those lacy things I like to take off you into a suitcase and leave the rest to me."

She said something under her breath, but the only word he caught was *men*. It was said in an exasperated tone of voice he'd heard from his sister enough times to know it wasn't an endearment, so he didn't press her to repeat it. Nor did he tell her he would change her mood to the one she'd been in the night before as soon as he walked in the door. He hadn't graduated at the top of his class in law school for nothing.

"I'll be with you in about fifteen minutes," he said calmly. "Then I'll help you whittle down the list. Okay?"

"Okay," she said with a sigh. After a short pause she said softly, "Turner?"

He closed his eyes as he was filled with a sweet ache for her. "I'm going to get a speeding ticket if you say my name like that again."

"Turner, be serious for a minute. This is important."

"Honey, I'm totally serious. When you say my name in that special soft way, all I can think about is seriously making love with you." Since the thought of sheathing himself in her warmth wasn't making driving the car particularly safe, he gave them both a break and asked, "What's so serious?"

"I'm usually a better sport than this."

He smiled. "Don't worry about it. Everything will work out. We'll make them work out."

After another pause she said, "There is something I need to know that isn't on the list but should be."

"What is it?"

"How are you going to introduce me to your father and brother? As your paralegal, your lover, a friend? How?"

"Well, I could say you're all three, which would be

the truth, but for accuracy's sake, I will introduce you as the love of my life."

She made an exasperated sound. "You can't say that."

Now he was grinning. "Why not? It's the truth." As enjoyable as it was to tease her, he put her out of her misery. "I plan to introduce you as the future Mrs. Turner Knight, which means King will probably embarrass me by turning cartwheels or firing off the fireworks he keeps on hand for special occasions."

If he hadn't heard her breathing, Turner would have thought she'd hung up. "Emma?"

"You never mentioned marriage before."

He frowned. Hadn't he? Apparently not. "Well, I'm certainly not going to propose to you on the phone. What would we tell our children? That thanks to AT and T their parents decided to make it legal?"

"Children?"

"For the sake of tradition, we'll have to give them Arthurian names, but as their middle names, not as their first names."

After yet another pause, Turner heard a strange tearing sound in the background. It was repeated one more time. "What was that?"

"The list," she replied calmly. "I just tore it up. It's not worth the paper it's printed on. I'm going to take your advice. While you're driving very carefully to get here I'm going to take a nice relaxing bubble bath and forget about having a quiet breakdown. I'll probably still be in the tub by the time you get here."

While visions of her silken skin covered with bubbles danced tantalizingly through his head, she added, "I'll save some bubbles for you."

With the added incentive Emma had just given him, Turner pressed his foot down on the accelerator.

Emma didn't think she'd be able to sleep with all there was to do, but after an inspired bout of lovemaking—which had resulted in a wet bathroom floor—she fell into a deep, restful sleep. Around two in the morning, however, something woke her.

A sweep of her arm over the other side of the bed told her she was alone. It was amazing how, in such a short time, she'd become so accustomed to sleeping with Turner that she woke up when he was no longer beside her. But what had made him get up?

Her first thought was that his ulcer had acted up again from the stress of getting ready to go to England. He'd been in an exceptionally good mood that night, even when he realized his skin smelled like gardenias from the bubble bath. But she knew Turner was also adept at handling stress by suppressing it, which was why he'd ended up with an ulcer in the first place.

She tossed back the cover and reached for something to wear. It turned out to be Turner's shirt. As she slipped her arms into the sleeves she saw a faint light through the gap left by the partially closed door. The direction of the shadows indicated the light was coming from her studio.

Her bare feet made no sound on the carpeted hall

floor as she left the bedroom and walked toward the source of the light. Turner was in the one room he had been in only once before.

Stopping in the doorway, she stared at the sight of Turner bent over the drawing table. He'd put on his jeans, but his back was bare as he sat on the stool, totally engrossed in whatever he was doing. She could hear the familiar soft scraping sound of a pencil on paper and wondered what he was working on.

Maybe this wasn't the best time to confront him about why he denied his artistic ability, she mused. On the other hand, the confrontation would be better now, before they flew to England, than when they returned. She instinctively felt that Turner's denial of his talent had something to do with his father.

She didn't have to announce her presence. Somehow he knew she was there.

Without looking up from the drawing board, he asked, "Are you going to stand there all night?"

"I might if you want to be left alone."

He turned on the stool and held out his hand. His smile was warm and intimate. "I've been lonely a long time and never knew it until I met you. Come here."

She grasped his hand and didn't resist when he drew her between his legs, kissed her, then turned her around to face the drawing board. Her breath caught in her throat when she saw what Turner had been drawing.

In front of her was a life-size drawing of her face and shoulders with Dragon in her arms. Emma felt her skin heat with a combination of embarrassment and desire when she recognized the look in her eyes. Love, passion, and a touch of humor were in her eyes and shaped her mouth.

"Do I really look at you like that?" she asked in an awestruck voice.

"Often enough to drive me crazy." His arms tightened around her waist, and he pulled her back against his chest. "Especially when we're in the office, where I can't do a damn thing about it."

She continued to stare down at the drawing. "Why tonight, Turner?" she asked quietly.

He'd bent his head to trail his mouth over her soft warm neck. "I was inspired."

His answer wasn't good enough. She loosened his arms and turned within their circle so she was facing him. "Why come in here tonight when you've continually denied your talent?"

The tension stiffening his spine was more from habit than from being defensive, Turner realized. With Emma, he didn't need to be anything other than who he was. That was the gift she'd given him. The woman he loved had given him back another love.

"Something Sadie said the other night kept coming back to me at odd times, buzzing around in my head like an irritating mosquito. She said that something you love isn't supposed to hurt you, that it should fulfill you and make you happy. Drawing and painting has been a part of me from the first time my father handed me a pencil and paper. It was like losing a vital organ when I gave it up."

"Why?" she asked. "Why give up something that means so much to you?"

"Out of some twisted loyalty to Dad, I put away my art supplies and chose law as a career."

She raised her hand to touch his face. "Your father, of all people, would understand your desire to paint."

He brought his hand up to cover hers, lacing their fingers together. "My father wasn't the problem. My pride was. I would have had to contend with being King Knight's son, live up to that at any art school I attended. If I turned out to be a good artist, I would feel I was in competition with my own father. If I ended up being a lousy artist, I wouldn't have been able to live with the knowledge I let him down."

"Do you really feel your father would consider you a failure no matter what you did? From what you've told me about your parents, they would continue to love and respect you if you chose to clean out monkey cages in a zoo."

His smile was a little off center. "You're probably right. But then you usually are."

"If I'm so smart, why haven't I been able to find the right words to convince you it's possible for you to be a lawyer and an artist? You don't have to sacrifice one for the other. You can have both. You need the law for that side of you that likes order and a challenge. Your incredible artistic ability shouldn't be wasted but used for your own pleasure."

He leaned his forehead against hers as a strange peace flowed over and around him.

Raising his head, he gazed down into her sable eyes. "I think you could make me believe anything." He cupped her face in his hands. "I've learned a great deal from you, Emma. Did you know that? You've taught me to live each day as though it's a gift that might be taken away. You've made me feel ashamed of having so much and wasting it when you had nothing and used every scrap of life you could clasp in your slender hands."

He heard her breathing quicken when he let his hands flow over her shoulders.

"And passion," he continued, his voice growing huskier. "I thought I knew all there was to know about sensuality, about sexual pleasure. Then you took me deeper into the realm of desire than I ever knew existed. I've never needed anyone like I need you."

She melted against him. "Oh, Turner."

"You've opened up a whole new world to me, Emma, and I don't want to live in it without you. I love you. I want you to marry me. It's the only way I can be sure you won't give me another two weeks' notice and leave me."

She closed her eyes for a moment and let his softly spoken declaration soak into her. "I love you, too, Turner, but I'm so afraid I'll disappoint you."

His initial reaction was to laugh because her fears were ridiculous. Instead he asked quietly, "What are you afraid of?"

She ran her tongue over her suddenly dry lips. "You know about my background. I haven't any experience with marriage, a family, raising children, or being a proper wife."

He smiled, his hands sliding down to her waist. "I wouldn't mind an improper wife, especially in the bedroom. Our life together will be whatever we want it to be, not the way others think it should be or some author with a bunch of degrees after their name says it should be. You have Sadie and I have King to bring to our marriage. Trust me, it's a fair exchange."

"I can't abandon Sadie, Gus, and the others."

"I wouldn't expect you to abandon them, although I'd rather you let me come with you when you visit them. Not everyone on the streets is like Sadie and Gus, and I would worry myself sick every time you went alone. It'll give me an opportunity to get on Sadie's good side. Somehow," he added with a martyred sigh, "I'm going to convince Sadie that this particular lawyer isn't the scum of the earth."

Emma wrapped her arms around his neck. "Letting her hold our first child might do it," she murmured, her eyes glowing with love and happiness.

The thought of Emma round with his child quickened his heart rate and rekindled the fire that always smoldered in his blood.

"Does that mean you'll marry me? You haven't said you would."

"I suppose I'd better," she said, smiling. "For the sake of the children."

"As the father of your future children, I feel it my duty to make sure you get plenty of rest."

He scooped her up in his arms and carried her out of the studio. The lamp over the drawing table was still on, but neither of them seemed to notice or care.

Turner lowered Emma onto the bed and came down to lie beside her. "I love you, Embrace."

She smiled and slid her arms around his neck to bring him down to her. "I love you, Lamorek."

He grinned. "There's just one more little thing to get out of the way."

She trailed her hand over his back, reveling in the strength under her fingers. "Couldn't we discuss whatever it is tomorrow?"

He shook his head as he unbuttoned his shirt, which she was wearing. "This will just take a minute. It's about your resignation from Kimball and Knight."

"What about it? Are you going to make me add another week after we get back from England since I won't be working this week while we're gone?"

"I wouldn't think of it," he said in a low rasping voice as he parted the front of his shirt and lowered his head. He took a budding nipple into his mouth and smiled when he heard her make a low sound of pleasure.

"You don't get to quit," he murmured, raising his head again to meet her eyes. "You're fired."

Emma choked back a laugh. "I can see where I'm going to have to buy a whole new set of books to learn how to play chess. You're always one move ahead of me."

He moved over her, parting her legs with his. "I think we're evenly matched in every way, but I'll show you an important move in chess. It's called taking the queen."

Emma closed her eyes as she felt him thrust within her.

"Checkmate," she sighed.

THE EDITOR'S CORNER

Come join the celebration next month when LOVE-SWEPT reaches its tenth anniversary! When the line was started, we made a very important change in the way romance was being published. At the time, most romance authors published under a pseudonym, but we were so proud of our authors that we wanted to give them the credit and personal recognition they deserved. Since then LOVESWEPT authors have always written under their own names and their pictures appear on the inside covers of the books.

Right from the beginning LOVESWEPT was at the cutting edge, and as our readership changes, we change with them. In the process, we have nurtured writing stars, not only for romance, but for the publishing industry as a whole. We're proud of LOVESWEPT and the authors whose words we have brought to countless readers over the last ten years.

The lineup next month is indeed something to be proud about, with romances from five authors who have been steady—and stellar—contributors to LOVESWEPT since the very beginning and one up-and-coming name. Further, each of these six books carries a special anniversary message from the author to you. So don't let the good times pass you by. Pick up all six books, then sit back and enjoy!

The first of these treasures is **WILDFIRE**, LOVE-SWEPT #618 by Billie Green. Nobody can set aflame a woman's passion like Tanner West. He's spent his life breaking the rules—and more than a few hearts—and makes being bad seem awfully good. Though small-town Texas lawyer Rae Anderson wants a man who'd care for her and give her children, she finds herself rising to Tanner's challenge to walk on the wild side. This breathtaking romance is just what you've come to expect from super-talented Billie!

Kay Hooper continues her *Men of Mysteries Past* series with **THE TROUBLE WITH JARED**, LOVESWEPT #619. Years before, Jared Chavalier had been obsessed by Danica Gray, but her career as a gemologist had driven them apart. Now she arrives in San Francisco to work on the Mysteries Past exhibit of jewelry and discovers Jared there. And with a dangerous thief afoot, Jared must risk all to protect the only woman he's ever loved. Kay pulls out all the stops with this utterly stunning love story.

WHAT EMILY WANTS, LOVESWEPT #620 by Fayrene Preston, shocks even Emily Stanton herself, but she accepts Jay Barrett's bargain—ten days of her company for the money she so desperately needs. The arrangement is supposed to be platonic, but Emily soon finds she'll do just about anything . . . except let herself fall in love with the man whose probing questions drive her into hiding the truth. Fayrene delivers an intensely emotional and riveting read with this different kind of romance.

'TIL WE MEET AGAIN, LOVESWEPT #621 by Helen Mittermeyer, brings Cole Whitford and Fidelia Peters together at a high school reunion years after she'd disappeared from his life. She's never told him the heartbreaking reason she'd left town, and once the silken web of memories ensnares them both, they have to decide whether to let the past divide them once more . . . or to admit to a love that time has made only more precious. Shimmering with heartfelt emotion, **'TIL WE MEET AGAIN** is Helen at her finest.

Romantic adventure has never been as spellbinding as **STAR-SPANGLED BRIDE**, LOVESWEPT #622 by Iris Johansen. When news station mogul Gabe Falkner is taken by terrorists, he doesn't expect anyone to come to his rescue, least of all a golden-haired angel. But photojournalist Ronnie Dalton would dare anything to set free the man who'd saved her from death years ago, the one man she's always adored, the only man she dares not love. Iris works her bestselling magic with this highly sensual romance.

Last is **THE DOCTOR TAKES A WIFE**, LOVESWEPT #623 by Kimberli Wagner. The doctor is Connor MacLeod, a giant of a Scot who pours all his emotions into his work, but whose heart doesn't come alive until he meets jockey Alix Benton. For the first time since the night her life was nearly ruined, Alix doesn't fear a man's touch. Then suspicious accidents begin to happen, and Connor must face the greatest danger to become Alix's hero. Kimberli brings her special touch of humor and sizzling desire to this terrific romance.

On sale this month from Bantam are four spectacular women's fiction novels. From *New York Times* bestselling author Amanda Quick comes **DANGEROUS**, a breathtaking tale of an impetuous miss— and a passion that leads to peril. Boldness draws Prudence Merryweather into one dangerous episode after another, while the notorious Earl of Angelstone finds himself torn between a raging hunger to possess her and a driving need to keep her safe.

Patricia Potter's new novel, **RENEGADE**, proves that she is a master storyteller of historical romance. Set during the tumultuous days right after the Civil War, **RENEGADE** is the passionate tale of Rhys Redding, the Welsh adventurer who first appeared in **LIGHT-NING** and Susannah Fallon, who must trust Rhys with her life while on a journey through the lawless South.

Pamela Simpson follows the success of **FORTUNE'S CHILD** with the contemporary novel **MIRROR, MIRROR**. When an unexpected inheritance entangles Alexandra Wyatt with a powerful family, Allie finds herself falling in love. And as she succumbs to Rafe Sloan's seductive power, she comes to suspect that he knows something of the murder she'd witnessed as a child.

In a dazzling debut, Geralyn Dawson delivers **THE TEXAN'S BRIDE**, the second book in Bantam's series of ONCE UPON A TIME romances. Katie Starr knows the rugged Texan is trouble the moment he steps into her father's inn, yet even as Branch is teasing his way into the lonely young widow's heart, Katie fears her secret would surely drive him away from her.

Also on sale this month in the Doubleday hardcover edition is **MOONLIGHT, MADNESS, AND MAGIC**, an anthology of original novellas by Suzanne Forster, Charlotte Hughes, and Olivia Rupprecht, in which a journal and a golden locket hold the secret to breaking an ancient family curse.

Happy reading!

With warmest wishes,

Nita Taublib

Nita Taublib
Associate Publisher

Don't miss these fabulous
Bantam
Women's Fiction
titles
on sale in APRIL

RENEGADE
by Patricia Potter
author of LIGHTNING and LAWLESS

MIRROR, MIRROR
by Pamela Simpson
author of FORTUNE'S CHILD

THE TEXAN'S BRIDE
by Geralyn Dawson

In hardcover from Doubleday,
MOONLIGHT,
MADNESS, AND MAGIC
by Suzanne Forster, Charlotte
Hughes, and Olivia Rupprecht

RENEGADE
by Patricia Potter
author of LIGHTNING and LAWLESS

From award-winning author Patricia Potter comes a new novel of romance and adventure, a passionate tale of a scoundrel who becomes a seeker of justice and the woman who tames his reckless heart.

When Rhys Redding is freed from a Confederate jail at the end of the Civil War by Susannah Fallon, he has no idea that she will demand that he take her across the lawless South to her home in Texas. As they travel the scarred, burned-out land, they feel the heat of passion's flame. . . .

She swam back to the shallow part of the river, where Rhys was sitting on the bank, watching. Dusk was giving way to night; stars blinked overhead while a quarter moon hung precariously in the sky. She couldn't see the expression on Rhys's face as she climbed the bank, but she sensed a certain wariness in him.

"You look like a river sprite," he said.

"I'm afraid to ask what a river sprite looks like."

"Much too appealing," he said softly. "We'd better get back."

She hesitated. She didn't want to leave this spot yet. "May I use your comb?"

Without a word, he reached inside one of the saddlebags next to him and pulled out a comb, watching as she ran it through her tangled hair and yanked impatiently on snarls.

Still silent, he took the comb from her and guided it through the snarls with a patience she would never have expected. There was an intimacy about the act, about the gentle way he touched her that made her senses swim.

She felt as if she were falling into a jar of warm honey. It felt so good, yet she could easily drown. She had been here before, in this warm, intimate world he and she created together, and she was suddenly afraid that he might leave her again, allow her to sink into oblivion.

He finished smoothing her hair, but his fingers lingered just a second longer against her face. She turned around to look up at him. "Rhys?"

"Hmm?" The sound was something between a groan and a sigh, and she knew he was experiencing the same onslaught of feelings.

She found herself leaning against him, sharing a warmth that came from belonging—and passion. She felt that passion in herself, in him. In the sudden sensitivity of her breasts that were pressed against him, in the growing hardness of his manhood. She swallowed hard against her reaction, against the compulsion to say things that might push him away again, or create a barrier she feared she could never breach.

"Susannah, you don't know what you're doing."

"You're wrong," she disagreed.

"You were once afraid of me," he reminded her.

"I think I'll always be a little afraid of you," she said honestly.

"Wise lady."

"But it doesn't seem to matter," she added.

"Foolish lady."

"I know."

"Oh bloody hell," he swore. "Save me from American women." Then turning toward her boots, he said, "You'd better put them on. I'll go on ahead."

"Rhys, will you stay with us? When we get to home to Texas? We . . . I . . . need you."

"You need me like you need the pox." His voice was light but there was a hint of steel to it.

"Is that why you keep running away?"

"I don't run away."

"Then stay." It was a challenge.

"I only said I would get you to Texas."

"Are you so eager to return to England?"

His only answer was silence, and again she wondered about his past, his life.

He turned around, and in two long strides, he was in front of her, his dark eyes stormy. He leaned down and kissed her, a hard, punishing kiss with no gentleness this time, only a violence that had no restraint. Susannah felt a new kind of fear then, that she had baited the wolf too long.

He wasn't giving her an opportunity to respond; he was merely taking in the roughest possible way. She remembered the coldness in him when he had almost killed the thief, and the cool analytical way he had gathered the thieves' belongings, without compassion for the previous owners.

Susannah realized he had been right weeks ago when he had told her she saw only what she wanted to see. And she was suddenly frightened, more frightened than she'd ever been in her life. Frightened of her own volatile feelings, frightened of the ruthlessness he was displaying.

As if he took a certain satisfaction in her fear and the way she started fighting him, he suddenly stepped back.

"Never tempt a wolf," he warned.

MIRROR, MIRROR
by Pamela Simpson
author of FORTUNE'S CHILD

*They are only fragments of a memory, flickering shards of shadow
and fear, but they fill Alexandra Wyatt with indescribable dread.
For somewhere in the deepest corners of her mind, the child in her
remembers . . . murder.*

*What was the truth behind the killing Allie witnessed? When an
unexpected inheritance entangles her with a powerful family she
never knew, she is suddenly thrust into a bitter fight for some of the
most spectacular property on the California coast. Allie finds herself
taking sides, making enemies, and falling in love—with a man who
seems both to want her, and to want her out of the way. . . .*

*He made no secret of his intentions—or his reckless desire. But
even as Allie succumbed to Rafe Sloan's seductive power and mys-
terious charm, even as she came to admire his passion for the land
and his determination to control its destiny, she suspected he knew
something of the terrible secret that shadowed her dreams. And then,
in the blackness of night and the pleasure of his arms, a new memory surfaced—one that brought back the past with a vengeance and
made Allie wonder if she'd ever leave Rafe's embrace alive. . . .*

The mood between them, the setting, the moment, grew increasingly erotic. While a cold breeze rustled the branches of the nearby trees, and water lapped at the rocky shore only a few hundred yards away, Rafe and Allie were warmed by the hot water of the Jacuzzi—and by a growing desire for each other.

Looking at him, sitting only a few feet from her, she was intensely aware of his body . . . his broad chest, covered with a mat of softly curling, dark hair . . . his muscled shoulders . . . and visible through the clear water, narrow hips and sinewy thighs. His body was hard and fit from years of back-breaking physical labor.

Everything about him was so completely masculine, yet when he reached out to take her hand, his touch was exquisitely gentle. His fingers played with her wedding band as he said, "One of the first things I noticed about you were your hands. The fingers are so long and slender, like a pianist or a surgeon. I couldn't understand why you weren't wearing a wedding ring. It seemed unbelievable that some man hadn't talked you into marriage."

Jerking her hand away, as if his touch burned her, she said shakily, "Someone did. But we didn't make it past the engagement."

"Why?"

She couldn't talk about Dennis. Especially to Rafe. She didn't want to reveal how vulnerable she'd felt when he'd hurt and humiliated her with his casual infidelities. Part of her still felt that there must have been something lacking in her to send him off in pursuit of other women. Surely, if she'd been lovable enough, attractive enough, he wouldn't have wanted anyone else.

Looking away, she said quietly, "It just didn't work out."

For a moment Rafe simply looked at her with a thoughtful expression. Then, to her chagrin, he reached out and lightly stroked her cheek. "You're a very special woman, Allie. He was a fool to let you go."

She shivered, as though from a chill. But she wasn't cold. She was suffused with a penetrating warmth that had nothing to do with the hot water, and everything to do with Rafe's touch.

"You're trembling," he whispered.

"The wind . . ." she began.

But he shook his head. "It's not the wind."

His hand moved up to her hair that shone burnished gold in the moonlight. He curled a strand around his fingertip, then let it slip through his fingers.

She didn't move. She couldn't. He had moved along the underwater bench, and was so close now she could feel the warmth of his breath on her cheek, could see the glint of passion in those dark eyes. His eyes were luminous in the moonlight, as they stared into her own, willing her to be still, to not pull away.

"*No.*" She wasn't sure if she spoke the word, or merely thought it. Either way, it didn't matter. What had been building between them, practically from the first moment they'd met, was too strong to be denied by a feeble protest.

His thumb ran across her lips, pulling gently at them so that they opened slightly.

"How could any man who's ever kissed these lips possibly let you go?" Rafe murmured.

She was barely breathing now, the rise and fall of her chest hardly perceptible. Her body was rigid as she fought with all her self-control to rein in her rebellious feelings.

His hands moved to her shoulders. She could feel the strength in those hard, callused hands. Rafe pulled her close. When she tried to hold back, to resist, he slipped one arm around her back, holding her against him, her breasts just brushing his chest.

"Allie," he whispered, and on his lips her name sounded like an endearment.

Her lips parted slightly to murmur a protest. But before she could speak, his mouth was on hers, tender yet persistent. Her lips parted even further, and when his tongue touched hers, the sensation of warmth she'd felt turned into a raging fire.

Without thinking, her hands went to his chest. But instead of pushing him away, her fingers curled in the tight mat of chest hair.

Rafe sighed with inexpressible pleasure as his lips finally left hers and moved to brush lightly across her cheek, her jaw, down the slender line of her throat. Then they returned to her mouth with a groan of desire that sent shivers up her spine.

His lips possessed hers again. This time, she didn't just sit passively. Her tongue met his, her lips pressed against his.

While one hand cupped her face, the other moved in slow circles under the water to caress her trembling breast, barely covered by the tight latex of the swimsuit. Allie leaned back against the tile rim of the Jacuzzi and half-closed her eyes as Rafe continued the warm, wet massage of her body.

His hand moved down to her stomach, continuing the erotic, circular movement. His touch, along with the sensuous feeling of the hot, swirling water, filled her with a sweet languor. Her entire being felt open, unguarded, yielding. She wanted to give herself to him, to hold nothing back . . .

THE TEXAN'S BRIDE
by Geralyn Dawson

From award-winning Geralyn Dawson comes this uniquely appealing tale that pits a sassy innkeeper's daughter against a hardened Texan searching for his brother's killer.

In the following preview, Branch and Katie confront each other for the first time—but not, fortunately for readers, for the last.

Hunching his shoulders against the elements, he trudged the short distance to the inn. When he pulled the door open, a gust of wind yanked it from his numbed fingers. The door banged against the log wall, and a good measure of the storm blew past him into the room.

A voice rang out above the clatter of tankards and whiskey-pitched conversations. "Shut the door, mister. We'd just as soon keep the weather on the outside if you don't mind."

Branch was tired and hungry. One thing he didn't want right now was to listen to some smart-mouthed fool. He shut the door and turned with a caustic remark on the tip of his tongue.

He swallowed his words, choking.

The source of the carping voice carried two dead squirrels by the tail, stood all of five feet tall, and wore a high-necked, long-sleeved calico dress that stretched tight across a positively bodacious bosom.

Branch stood there, staring at the barmaid. "Well, well,

well," he drawled, "but couldn't you turn a blue norther red hot, little honey." He wouldn't mind a bit scorching some sheets with her a little later.

She glared at him through narrowed, bluebonnet-colored eyes. A flush crept over highly placed cheekbones, painting her fair skin an appealing pink beneath the light dusting of freckles. A long auburn braid fell over a shoulder. She tightened her full lower lip into an angry frown.

I wonder what's rattled her slats, Branch thought as his gaze swept her body before lifting to fasten on her chest. A blaze of lust melted the norther's chill from his bones. Plenty of curves for such a tiny package.

He was somewhat surprised at his reaction to this little bundle of femininity. He'd not dallied with a tavern chippy in years. Although never a man to shut his eyes when offered a spectacular view, he'd always looked for more in a woman than mere physical appeal. In this case, however, he desired to search no farther than the obvious set of features that even now approached.

A slow grin spread across his face as she walked toward him. He never lifted his stare above her neck. I do believe I'd rather watch her walk than eat fried chicken, he decided.

She stopped less than an arm's length away. He vaguely noticed the tapping sound her foot made against the puncheon floor; he was fascinated by the effect such a movement created.

She caught him completely by surprise and square in the face when she slapped him with the two dead squirrels.

"Thunder in the valley, woman!" Branch raged. He backed up a step and wiped his face with a corner of his coat. The blasted squirrels left something wet behind.

She dropped the animals and, with hands on hips, moved forward. He felt the wall against his back. Why, she wasn't the least bit cowed by his bellow, he realized. Male pride reasserting itself, he put *his* hands on *his* hips and leaned forward. Glaring down at her upturned face, he growled through clenched teeth. "What in Sam Houston's name do you think you're doin'?"

She punctuated her words with a surprisingly powerful jab to his chest with her index finger. "I think, mister, that you had best keep your eyes to yourself, or you'll be back out in the sleet looking about as healthy as these squirrels."

Branch shook his head in amazement. Nobody, especially not a hundred-pound little-bit, had dared to pull a stunt like this on him since his voice stopped cracking.

The only sound he heard was the slurping of ale as the occupants of the room watched the confrontation with rapt attention. He wondered what would happen if he gave the tiny termagant what she so obviously needed. He decided to settle for less, for now. What he had in mind required more privacy than the tavern presently offered.

He brought his right hand to his chest, rubbing the spot she had stabbed. His left hand snaked out to grab her wrist. Angry blue eyes widened at his action, and trepidation glimmered across her face. So she does have some sense after all, he thought, and grinned.

He looked deep into her eyes. Loosening his grip, he slid his hand over hers in a gentle caress until he held only her fingertips. He bowed low and pressed a honeyed kiss to the back of her hand. "I humbly beg your pardon, ma'am," he said in a loud voice. "I fear the bitter cold must have affected my sense. I acted the rogue and I apologize."

She tugged on her hand but he held it tight. In a lowered voice only she could hear, he continued, "One thing though, Sprite. From here on out, I do all the pokin'."

With a gasp, she yanked her hand away as though burned. She whirled and darted toward the exit. Branch laughed aloud when she stopped short at the doorway, turned, and marched back to retrieve her squirrels. With her perky nose high in the air, she flounced outside, not even bothering to don a cloak. The door slammed behind her.

OFFICIAL RULES TO WINNERS CLASSIC SWEEPSTAKES

No Purchase necessary. To enter the sweepstakes follow instructions found elsewhere in this offer. You can also enter the sweepstakes by hand printing your name, address, city, state and zip code on a 3" x 5" piece of paper and mailing it to: Winners Classic Sweepstakes, P.O. Box 785, Gibbstown, NJ 08027. Mail each entry separately. Sweepstakes begins 12/1/91. Entries must be received by 6/1/93. Some presentations of this sweepstakes may feature a deadline for the Early Bird prize. If the offer you receive does, then to be eligible for the Early Bird prize your entry must be received according to the Early Bird date specified. Not responsible for lost, late, damaged, misdirected, illegible or postage due mail. Mechanically reproduced entries are not eligible. All entries become property of the sponsor and will not be returned.

Prize Selection/Validations: Winners will be selected in random drawings on or about 7/30/93, by VENTURA ASSOCIATES, INC., an independent judging organization whose decisions are final. Odds of winning are determined by total number of entries received. Circulation of this sweepstakes is estimated not to exceed 200 million. Entrants need not be present to win. All prizes are guaranteed to be awarded and delivered to winners. Winners will be notified by mail and may be required to complete an affidavit of eligibility and release of liability which must be returned within 14 days of date of notification or alternate winners will be selected. Any guest of a trip winner will also be required to execute a release of liability. Any prize notification letter or any prize returned to a participating sponsor, Bantam Doubleday Dell Publishing Group, Inc., its participating divisions or subsidiaries, or VENTURA ASSOCIATES, INC. as undeliverable will be awarded to an alternate winner. Prizes are not transferable. No multiple prize winners except as may be necessary due to unavailability, in which case a prize of equal or greater value will be awarded. Prizes will be awarded approximately 90 days after the drawing. All taxes, automobile license and registration fees, if applicable, are the sole responsibility of the winners. Entry constitutes permission (except where prohibited) to use winners' names and likenesses for publicity purposes without further or other compensation.

Participation: This sweepstakes is open to residents of the United States and Canada, except for the province of Quebec. This sweepstakes is sponsored by Bantam Doubleday Dell Publishing Group, Inc. (BDD), 666 Fifth Avenue, New York, NY 10103. Versions of this sweepstakes with different graphics will be offered in conjunction with various solicitations or promotions by different subsidiaries and divisions of BDD. Employees and their families of BDD, its division, subsidiaries, advertising agencies, and VENTURA ASSOCIATES, INC., are not eligible.

Canadian residents, in order to win, must first correctly answer a time limited arithmetical skill testing question. Void in Quebec and wherever prohibited or restricted by law. Subject to all federal, state, local and provincial laws and regulations.

Prizes: The following values for prizes are determined by the manufacturers' suggested retail prices or by what these items are currently known to be selling for at the time this offer was published. Approximate retail values include handling and delivery of prizes. Estimated maximum retail value of prizes: 1 Grand Prize ($27,500 if merchandise or $25,000 Cash); 1 First Prize ($3,000); 5 Second Prizes ($400 each); 35 Third Prizes ($100 each); 1,000 Fourth Prizes ($9.00 each) ; 1 Early Bird Prize ($5,000); Total approximate maximum retail value is $50,000. Winners will have the option of selecting any prize offered at level won. Automobile winner must have a valid driver's license at the time the car is awarded. Trips are subject to space and departure availability. Certain black-out dates may apply. Travel must be completed within one year from the time the prize is awarded. Minors must be accompanied by an adult. Prizes won by minors will be awarded in the name of parent or legal guardian.

For a list of Major Prize Winners (available after 7/30/93): send a self-addressed, stamped envelope entirely separate from your entry to: Winners Classic Sweepstakes Winners, P.O. Box 825, Gibbstown, NJ 08027. Requests must be received by 6/1/93. DO NOT SEND ANY OTHER CORRESPONDENCE TO THIS P.O. BOX.